See yourself in

Pink Shorts

Reginald Lee Hameth

Bloomington, IN   authorHOUSE®   Milton Keynes, UK

AuthorHouse™
1663 Liberty Drive, Suite 200
Bloomington, IN 47403
www.authorhouse.com
Phone: 1-800-839-8640

AuthorHouse™ UK Ltd.
500 Avebury Boulevard
Central Milton Keynes, MK9 2BE
www.authorhouse.co.uk
Phone: 08001974150

This book is a work of fiction. People, places, events, and situations are the product of the author's imagination. Any resemblance to actual persons, living or dead, or historical events, is purely coincidental.

First published by AuthorHouse 12/12/2006

ISBN: 978-1-4259-8562-2 (sc)

Printed in the United States of America
Bloomington, Indiana

This book is printed on acid-free paper.

To my wife, Regina and my daughter, Haley
Thank you for loving and supporting me. I love you.

Table of Contents

The Accountant

I had worn a hole in my routine and my life although perfect on the surface was empty. After marrying a doctor and having two beautiful children, I felt I was well on my way to the thrill of a lifetime. Unfortunately, my passion for life had lost its way and somewhere between the private school drops and daily bean counting, my passion screamed rescue me.

After a long talk with some of my girlfriends over the weekend, I began thinking about how we used to meet at happy hour all over the city and enjoy the weekly stories about how guys' souls would tremble when we entered the room. We all agreed that fifteen pounds and fifteen years later, the respondents were fewer and older. What was worse I had begun to dress as conservatively as I felt yet the relentless passion inside urged my spirit to spread its wings.

Monday morning began for me the same as it had the previous five years by getting the kids up, greeting the husband in the kitchen for a sip of coffee and an air kiss, school drops, and straight to my cubicle. I had become the poster child for another day another dollar. As the woman in me wilted away, the sound of footsteps and unfamiliar voices grabbed my attention long enough for me to give the keyboard a break. As I turned my chair, I locked eyes with a man that made my body ache in sweet ways it had not done in years. Blushing as if he had seen me naked, I quickly answered my phone that did not even ring. I could not believe how the mere sight of the man caused me to embarrass myself like that. The only thing more embarrassing than me acting like a silly schoolgirl was the fact that the on-the-surface superman was about to start his first job after college, wow! This had to be the guy that all the women in the office were talking about last week. I had never heard so many stories about what they would do to him if they had the chance. After seeing him for myself, I certainly understood why.

Although I had only worked for this firm for five years, I had fifteen years of experience and was often asked to train new employees. As the good and bad within me began a fierce battle to dominate my mind, it became clear to me that in my mind the days of the happy hour could return for me. Only this time, I would be the one whose soul would tremble. As the anticipation became unbearable, the assignment was given to me. My boss proudly said, "Rachel, this is Mark. He will be assigned to you for phase 1 training."

As I stood to greet my boss and meet the man who minutes earlier penetrated everything feminine within me, I regained my composure and extended a firm corporate grip that veiled my raunchy mindset. I said, "I will take good care of Mark." In my mind, what normally would have been an older woman mentoring a younger man, a transformation had taken place. I found myself attracted to this man and not in an I-can-introduce-him-to-my niece kind of way.

The first day we worked together, I was my usual stuffy self but as we became more comfortable with each other, we relaxed. By day four, I was relaxed enough to wear my contacts instead of glasses. I even wore my hair down and showed my cleavage that day. I noticed that Mark was distant for some reason.

That evening after everyone left, I asked him if everything was ok. He mentioned that he had something on his mind but he didn't think it would be appropriate to share with me because it could jeopardize his career. Being the more mature one, I knew that he needed reassurance that it would be ok to speak freely. I smiled and said sweetly, "I want to know."

Mark asked me to stand as he moved slowly into my sacred space. The city's skyline set the mood for the moment my mind created when I first saw him. Little did I know that sixty-nine floors above the earth could feel so close to heaven. Mark looked deeply into my eyes and said, "Rachel, this is what I have been thinking. When you walked in this morning, I thought, there is the woman I saw when our eyes locked the first time we saw each other. I hope that at the end of the night I will be standing face-to-face with her sharing this. It looks like we made it."

As I stood before him wondering and hoping there would be more, he delivered. After confidently asking me to close my eyes, I did so without hesitation. I closed my eyes to the world and stood willingly before the marvelous sexy man. I felt him moving about only to resurface behind me with his lips just inches away from my neck and his obviously expanding manhood stretching towards my smooth cheeks that were nearly visible through my thin skirt. As I slid my hair to the side, my body starved for his masculine touch. As he moved closer, the warmth of his breath on my neck caused the warm water in my pink river to overflow. Suddenly, I heard his deep voice speaking softly into my ear, he said, "My spirit wants to love your spirit tonight."

I felt his strong hands slither around my waist with the skill of a man at least fifteen years older. I ached with anticipation. As his warm mouth ignited me from my neck down, a manifestation of my warmth clouded what was a clear vision of the city's skyline. The more he pressed his firm masculinity against my surrendering body the louder my breathing became. As our intimate journey continued, my handprints on the sixty-ninth floor window marked the spot that would bridge our generational taboos. As his strong palms tenderly massaged the flesh of my melting body, my feminine honey overflowed into my cute panties. Little did he know that he created a remnant that he would enjoy long after that night. I figured he deserved to own the masterpiece that his touch painted with my body's honey. Without looking back, everything in me begged him to enter my wet world and love me with the power of nature. No sooner than I could get the thought out of my head, my body quaked and my tide rose as the winds within my soul swirled with a sweet violent twist that weakened my burning body. His manhood and my womanhood were entangled in an erotic slow grind sixty-nine floors above the city. Suddenly, I opened eyes only to find out that I was standing next to my cubicle and not against the window.

Only then did I realize that the man had only whispered everything that I imagined in my ear. He respectfully stroked my soul from a distance. I stood in frozen silence. I turned slowly just to get a glimpse of his silhouette leaving the room. After a few minutes, I had to sit down and get myself together. Just as I lifted my briefcase from my desk, I noticed a note written on one of my spreadsheets. It read, "When spirits touch, nothing else has to."

The Bartender

As I tossed my graduation cap into the air, I fought back the celebratory tears that would ultimately crawl down my officially an adult face. The excitement of knowing how proud my parents were of their sassy cutie who just topped her graduation class and sealed a deal with the suits reduced their streetwise scholar into a sweet little girl who made her parents proud. My myth destroying ascension was a prelude to a series of myths that would be challenged over the next couple of years of my life.

Although I was offered an outstanding position with my new employer months prior, the location of my assignment had not yet been determined. As I sat nervously awaiting the call, I thought about how nice it would be to work in Atlanta, DC, or New York. Well, the call came and when I heard that I would be starting at the company's newest location in the Mountain West Region, I nearly dropped the phone. After a few seconds of awkward silence, I uttered my first politically correct words, "I am looking forward to the assignment." I gathered myself and regained the confidence that had gotten me that far. I figured it would not be so bad seeing another side of the world for a change. A change is exactly what I experienced.

When I exited the plane, I felt eyes piercing me. Now, don't get me wrong I was use to getting that kind of attention because I am quite easy on the eyes. However, the attention, this time, probably had more to do with my tone than my stunning looks. As I strutted with my head held high, I owned the terminal-turned-runway. I could not help but chuckle as the guys who would be disowned by their families tried to sneak a peek as my presence temporarily broadened their horizons. Of course, the reception from their lady friends was less than warm. I thought, wow, this is going to be interesting.

After spending a few weeks being acclimated to my new surroundings, I knew that I had to find something, hell anything, to make the place worthwhile. Lord knows if I had to field another cultural question about something my co-workers saw on television, I would be terminated and perhaps incarcerated. Suddenly, I started to think about some of the benefits my company offered and then it hit me. They will pay for graduate school! After all, just like in my childhood, school always took my mind off my surroundings.

A few weeks later after completing my enrollment into graduate school, my life began to take on a comfortable routine but something was still missing. I realized that all I did was work and study so I needed to inject some playtime into my life. I started thinking about how I enjoyed people watching so I narrowed my choices to bartending at a spot just outside of town. I thought what could be more interesting than seeing my new world in such a spirited environment. It turns out that environment was more interesting than I imagined.

Three months after blending into my new element, the community embraced me as if I were a beautiful rare species. The stares that came months before reinvented themselves and became warms eyes of affection. In their eyes, I had become one of them. As the tips poured in and the conversations became more frequent, I felt right at home. The stage was set and the curtain on my new world was opening slowly.

A regular crew of loggers and truckers became my bar stool patients as they poured out their lives to me between drinks. I could always expect a nice tip from my guys. Hell, I deserved it after listening to all of that crap. These guys kept me smiling all the time with lame comments about how cute and sexy I was. It was all in fun because they knew they did not have a chance in hell of getting their rugged asses anywhere near me. Laughing it up with these guys was just the release I needed to unwind from a long day of work and school. While my regular crew was loud and boisterous, another crew did not say much but I would always get a twenty-dollar bill with a heart drawn on it from their table. The first few times it happened I didn't think much of it but when it started to happen two or three times a week, I became nervous and kind of excited at the same time.

As I lay in bed one night, I realized that it had been months since I had felt the touch of masculinity. I was so into my new job, graduate school, and my new surroundings, I temporarily lost the woman in me. Now, being as real as I am I quickly found the woman in me that night without the masculine touch. With sticky sweet fingers, I lovingly tucked myself into the warm covers as my honey-sweet scent blessed my soft sheets. The woman in me was alive and the next day I found out just how alive she was.

Little did I know that my kinky behavior from the night before would only create an urge that would test me in ways I had never experienced. I put on the sexiest suit I had in my closet and headed for work. With every step through the workplace, I felt eyes undressing me. As my confidence skyrocketed even more, my feminine center quivered. I could not believe how turned on I was. I needed more attention so I decided to stop by the bar only this time I was a customer.

When I walked into the bar, I heard more screams, claps, and hollers than I had ever heard. By that time, I had taken off my hose and showcased my smooth legs for the lusting crowd. I walked right up to the bar and sat down next to some of the guys. Before I could get my drink, a tap on my shoulder interrupted my conversation. As I turned, a cap-wearing stranger gave me a neatly folded bill. He looked like he should be on a runway instead of a bar in the mountains. He walked away before I could even thank him. When I unfolded the bill, I knew then that I had just come face-to-face with my mystery man. I got up and walked around to find him so I could thank him but my search ended in disappointment.

After the crowd started to thin, I decided to help Sarah close the place. As we began, shutting things down, she received a call from her mother telling her that her child was sick. I told her to go and I would finish closing. After closing, I began studying to try to take my mind off my starving womanhood. It was not working too well. I even started listening to cars as they rolled by every ten minutes or so. That did not last long so I studied more. As my studies extended my already stretched day, I noticed a truck with a local company's name on the side pull into a parking space. Apparently, whoever it was noticed my car and thought we were still open. As my tired eyes peered through the door, ready to greet the soon-to- be disappointed visitor, a towering hunk of a man moved towards the door. Something in me was so excited to see the man but I had to remain calm. I may have appeared calm on the surface but the woman behind calm was having thoughts like she never had. Never had I been so turned on by someone worlds apart from me.

Feeling comfortable enough to allow him to come in I introduced myself. I nervously uttered, "I'm Imani." He replied, "I'm John." His huge hand completely covered my small hand as our skin met for the first time. I offered to make him a drink but he refused and insisted on making us both a drink. While I grabbed a seat at the bar, he did his best impression of a bartender. It was actually quite nice watching him serve me. I told him before I could chat with him I needed to study one more page. As I took my seat on top of the bar where my books were spread, he sat on a bar stool and watched me study as he sipped on his drink. Finally, I finished studying and with the slam of my textbook, my lips touched John's drink for the first time. It was a delicious prelude.

After exchanging life stories and aspirations with him, I decided to lay back and close my eyes and let his sweet beverage move through my system to heighten my sensation. It felt so good to have his creation inside of me. I took my shoes off and released a sexy sigh of relief. As awkward silence crept into our otherwise easy flowing evening, our attraction bridged the gap. Suddenly, I felt his hands caressing my feet and it felt like someone was rubbing warm silk wrapped in love on every nerve in my body. With my eyes still closed, I relaxed and let this man behind my eyelids be just that, a man. He moved onto the bar and knelt before me. My body quivered with anticipation as he lifted my feet to his chiseled chest. Moving my feet up to his mouth, he kissed my pretty feet gently as my inner fire raged. After teasing my feet with his tongue, he moved my feet slowly down to his myth-destroying manhood. I was like, damn! I could hear his heavy breathing increase as my peds prepared him to enter an unfamiliar world. What he did next weakened my body. His soft tongue found its way to my lady river and without completely removing my honey-soaked panties, he touched my soul as I slowly squirmed to try to escape the reality. He quenched his thirst with my body's succulent nectar. Just when I did not think I could further lose myself in the moment of my changing world, our 'hoods came together, my womanhood and his manhood. As his rugged mountainous masculinity penetrated my tender urban sweetness, each myth-shattering stroke struck a sweet chord that blended us like Neapolitan. Together, we were a perfect melody and our different worlds danced an explosive passionate two-step for the first time. We knew that the music of our blended dance could wake our generations but that night we did not care. That night we let our music play until our exhausted bodies tenderly collapsed and melted into one another.

Over the next couple of months, John and I kept everything on a friendship level. We never spoke about the night our worlds became one. One day while we were chatting, I got a call from my boss informing me that he had an opportunity for me in Atlanta and the assignment would start in two weeks. I was thrilled and I immediately shared the good news with John. He wished me well and took out his trademark twenty-dollar bill and gave it to me. I put the money in my purse and walked away locking away my to-the-grave secret with every step.

The Congresswoman

After a successful stint as one of the state's brightest political stars, I knew that my calling was higher and that I could not rest until I followed my passion. I knew before I stepped onto a college campus that I would be a political science major. With all the crap involved in politics, I must have been out of my mind to pursue such a career. There are times, even now, when I ask myself "What the hell was I thinking?" I knew when I started my quest that I would need a strong support system around me. I aligned my team using the best-of-the-best. People who had been in my personal and my professional corners for years built a fortress around me to shield against the firestorm of political tricks that would come with my boldest aspiration to date.

My most impressive team member was my campaign manager. The man took a sabbatical from his world to help me with mine. Aside from his selflessness, he had a look that would surely capture the feminine vote if I placed him on my campaign poster. I was really looking forward to working with the former pro athlete who looks like he could score right now. During the campaign, I could tell there were several high hems that wanted him to test that theory.

Well, anyway, there I was standing before the media about to announce my candidacy for a U.S. congressional seat. As the reporters readied their questions and the cameras were positioned, the moment of truth arrived and it was time to put on a show. On cue, my pearly white smile petitioned millions with the hope that on Election Day that screen's image would be the same. After the announcement, it was time to go to work. Considering my opponent who represented the district for several years with the support of the entire community, I knew that I had to run an effective and most of all respectful campaign.

Like a chameleon, the ever-changing face of the community recreation center was transformed into the most important springboard of my life. As I reflected on my childhood days in the community, I got a little misty. From the same floor that once served as my play area stood a sexy well-to-do icon whose name was synonymous with success. I knew that hard work was the key to my success but I had to play just as hard to maintain balance. That play area created memories of a different kind thirty years later.

My first day began with a staff meeting. When I walked in it came as no surprise that the friendly yet strong feminine instincts were in full-effect. You should have seen how these little heifers were dressed in the sexiest borderline attire they could find. Being a brilliant secure diva, I took center stage in the spot that would house my campaign's masculine marvel for the next few months. When I walked past his office, before I said good morning, I took a couple of seconds to take a mental snap shot of his backside as he climbed the ladder to hang the banner. "Whew!" I said quietly to myself. As he looked over his shoulder and noticed my direction-changing eyes, he blushed and said, "Good morning." His voice sounded like pillow talk. I gave him a sexy glare that synchronized my womanhood and his manhood. He said, "Don't start." Bursting into laughter like school kids, we agreed to start the meeting in ten minutes.

At the start of the meeting, it was easy to see who would be in charge of this show so I sat back and watched him work his magic. Since I had known him for some time, I was accustomed to seeing him in action. Now, the others had not had the pleasure of working directly with him so they watched in awe. I, on the other hand, watched him through lustful eyes that created a mental path that slowly inched its way down to the woman in me. As my mind began a separate campaign to pull him into my on-the-spot fantasy, my sweet signal of pheromones billowed towards his primal masculinity and drew his waistline directly into my line of vision. I felt a little guilty as I watched nature control the fine specimen. As his strong hands massaged the back of my leather chair with each passionate point, I grasped every commanding word when he stepped to the side of me to further his point. As he laid out his plan, others looked on with envy as they wished they were in my seat. As my posture revealed my hidden campaign, I quickly snapped back to the reason we were there and my professionalism regained its rightful place.

As the weeks rolled on, the name Sylvia Jones-Massey held its own in the trenches. I watched my team work tirelessly to make my dream a reality. Because this awesome team was there on the frontline for me dispelling any rumors about their golden child, I made sure that I thanked them every day. I watched the ladies work through lunch, work on weekends, and roll up their sleeves for me. While they stepped up in a big way, my campaign manager worked harder than anyone. In many cases, the man would not leave the headquarters until 2:00 am only to return four hours later. He even listened to my tear-laced voice on nights when the pressure was overwhelming and somewhere between the comfort of his exhausted voice and phone line from headquarters to my home, his care wiped away my tears. For weeks, he was a tender loving ghost in my world.

The last Friday before the election was upon us so it was time for me to give my staff a treat. After the busiest week ever, I could not wait to thank my staff for putting their all into my campaign. I decided to take everyone to dinner at the city's newest bistro. Screams of joy filled the room as they simultaneously opened their envelopes and unveiled an all-inclusive cruise courtesy of their soon-to-be congresswoman. Of course, I am no fool so I paid for each vacation separately out of my personal account just in case those in the political circle had something to say about it. As for my dynamic campaign manager, I winked and said, "You'll get yours later, sir." With that, everyone finished their desserts and headed home.

The next three days were a blur as everyone went into overdrive. After appearing everywhere I could to get that last reminder out to the public, the moment arrived. As the results started to come in, I was a little nervous. I was slightly behind but only forty percent of the precincts had reported. I guess it showed on my face because my campaign manager gripped my hand tightly and whispered words of encouragement. I regained my composure and stood ready to accept the outcome. As the results came in cheers erupted throughout my headquarters. Confetti blended with screams of joy, hugs, and celebratory music opened the door to world of Congresswoman Sylvia Jones-Massey!

As the camera lights and champagne temporarily blinded me, my desired camera image was not the same as I hoped it would be when the campaign started but it no longer mattered. After thanking the voters and everyone under the sun, I was ready to collapse but I had one more thing to do. As the patriotic confetti and crumpled posters covered the floor, I breathed a sigh of relief and fell into his arms. I was so glad that everyone was finally gone. I went into the kitchen and got the last bottle of champagne so I could have a toast to victory with the man behind my campaign. I could not believe that when I walked into his office he was on the ladder removing a banner. I shook my head and said, "Relax baby, it's over." I walked over to him and offered him a glass and with a toast, the first of many of the night's sips began. I took him by the hand and said, "You have worked hard enough. It's my turn." Before he could sit down, I was standing in front of him ready to give him the woman in me from every angle. Using the remote, I turned the carousel to a disc filled with slow passionate jazz. As the music played, I peeled off stitch after stitch revealing what looked like the body I had when we met. He wanted to touch me but I would not let him. He quickly understood that his work was done and I was now in charge. My sexy lace panties were all that covered my gorgeous body. I could see the fire in his eyes for me as I leaned into him with a stripper-like tease. My scent intoxicated his airways as his primal side awakened. As I rotated my sweet hips on the crotch of his tailored suit, his throb desperately pressed against me, but I pressed down even more as my body asked him if he really wanted it. As our high school-like grind intensified, I slithered down his leg gently nibbling on his bulge as I passed. With a rhythmic flick of my wrist, I unzipped him and revealed his powerful manhood. I immediately placed my starving mouth onto his masculine center and loved it until the rest of his body begged for mercy. With each warm silky stroke, his veins expanded my already stretched mouth and it was my pleasure. Just when it became unbearable for him, I stopped and like a movie in reverse, I slithered back to my original lap-loving position and slowly removed the candy-soaked lace.

With that, my pink sweetness melted onto him and sprinkled dew drops of lust onto his pubic forest. Every fantasy I ever had about the man resurfaced with each gripping stroke. I fought my body and mind desperately to hold back the manifestation of the fantasies. My mind and body lost the battle as I shattered within and sent waves of ecstasy to my surface. After collapsing in his arms and basking in the moment, I finally gathered enough strength to say, "Mr. Massey, let's finish in our bed."

The DJ

reached the pinnacle of success in my small community and I knew that soaring into my dream meant tears for many including me. For more than a year, my mind wrestled with love. What I had to figure out was which love was stronger the love for myself or the love for those who were kind enough to lend me their ears for more than a decade. With faith wiping away my good-bye tears, I soared into my dream. Within my dream, I found a sobering reality that changed my position in life's line of opportunity.

With the door to my new world getting closer, the static faded enough to allow me to a sample the station's smooth format. I knew that coming from a smaller market I would have to put my illustrious small-market career in a mental memory book because in my new city I was an unknown. Unaccustomed to anonymity, I felt an intern-like fire burning. I put on my game face and a damn cute game face I might add. Mentally prepared, I exited the interstate and followed the road that would ultimately become an exhilarating road to success.

I was exhausted after the ten-hour drive. I was even too tired to unload the rest of my things. As I entered the door to my condo, I had to step over boxes just to get to my couch that would serve as my bed for the night. At 6:00 am, a smooth bass-laden sunrise gently kissed my eardrums and welcomed me to the city. As the words flowed from his lips and embraced my morning, my hand froze in mid-air because snooze was not an option. I could not wait to meet the man attached to that voice. I knew that the station's format was smooth but wow! After spending a few moments, lusting after his voice, I finally made it to the shower and let the warm water love my feminine nerves like an aquatic toy. It was just the touch I needed to get my day started right.

When I entered the parking lot, I did not see a space reserved for me. The reminders of not being the top personality were adding fuel to my fire. I was determined to take the station and the city by storm. As the left tip of my stylish dress sandal touched the ground of my new environment, I noticed the parking lot security guard staring unapologetically as the rest of me emerged from my sporty red two-seater. He just elevated me to his top personality for sure but I had more work to do. I strutted into the office leaving a sweet-scented trail that left curious workers in a daze. I was ready to ease into my slot. As I sat before the station manager, I could tell I was not the only one who wanted to ease into my slot. Unfortunately, for him, my mind was elsewhere in the station. Looking at the time, I grew concerned as to whether or not I would have the pleasure of hearing the voice man's strong pipes offer me a personalized greeting. As my invisible honey sweetened the corridors of my new workplace, I could see the consensus through their lusting eyes. The duality of my appeal spared no one. Even a shorthaired skirt or two had hopeful visions as I displayed all that I will ever be to them, a distant tease.

Fortunately, for me, my station manager had to run to a meeting and my guided tour was over so I entered the studio alone. There he was the owner of the voice that renewed my ears' virginity. I had never heard anything like it. His voice was the epitome of masculinity and every time I heard it, my nerves of pleasure wanted to explode. His voice-matching face could not hide the body-melting emotions he felt the moment he saw me. His hand was not the only thing he extended to me as I watched his nervous legs butterfly inward and squeeze his salute to me. With a smiling voice, he introduced me to his listeners with the pride of a newlywed. As my feminine equivalent to his panty-soaking voice laced the airwaves for the first time in my new world, I felt like I was whispering individual fantasies to every male listener. A teasing audio ménage was in full effect as together we soaked and stiffened the listeners during my introduction. As the hour's final song brought closure, his cologne massaged my airways as our personal space diminished with the melody of fading music. Our body language spoke for us as the ambiance controlled us. Just inches away from each other, unspoken words from both of our eyes kept our kiss mental.

After the show, we composed ourselves and awkwardly converted the conversation to my career, my new city, and the happening spots. He even offered to take me on a tour of the city once I got settled but I declined because, even though he was a delicious sight, I did not want to jump on or into him too fast. I decided that I would explore the new world alone. After all, I would see plenty of him at the station. As I reversed my path to say nice to meet you to more than a few, I decided to work my gym-prepared behind with every step. I realized that I had just dropped some sweet feminine poison in the minds of many including the station's would-be king. I knew that if I let him, he would sin in unimaginable ways with me. The power of sexy had them panting and their bodies pulsating. The stage was set for a jazz show like no other.

Since, I would not officially start work until the following week, it was time for me to see my surroundings. As I left the building, I decided to walk a few blocks. I noticed some essentials, a coffee shop, a gym, and a mall. With my basic three in striking distance, I mentally mapped out my soon-to-be daily routine. For the next few days, I spent time running errands and making sure my home was in order. I even hit the gym a couple of times to make sure the temple remained intact. I even saw the voice man as he tried to pretend he was just having a casual conversation with a scantily clad cutie. When I stopped to say hello, I made sure I hugged him like we had known each other for years. He gripped me tightly much to the chagrin of his lady friend. When he introduced us, my coworker title did little to hide her sudden attitude as she offered a less than warm greeting. I told him that I would see him later at the station.

For the next few months, I started to make a name for myself over the airwaves by working all time slots. It was like being on call as my station manager became quite familiar with my cell number. It was a little different for me but it was ok because I knew my day was coming. It was worth it because listeners started to recognize me around town. My niche was slowly being carved and it felt so good. The voice man even noticed my independence as his starving eyes signified an even stronger attraction to me. As he humbled himself, his desire to be around me increased. Not only was he attracted to me physically, he was now attracted to the attention that now came with me.

After becoming a regular quiet storm personality due to the departure of a former host, my schedule became a normal one. The best part about it was that my night would kiss his morning five times a week. Like clockwork, our days blended well. He would even bring coffee in the morning just to warm my day. With the change in season, I appreciated that coffee even more because the city's coats were now unpacked.

One night as the cold wet weather hindered the city, my music allowed me to escape to a place in my mind where the fire was a few feet away and my body was wrapped in strong arms of passion. Something in the music that night stroked my mind and massaged my sweet divide. My femininity was raging as I made love to my listeners through creamy soothing words that poured slowly into the microphone. As evidenced by the disproportionate number of male callers that night, my show was strip teasing for their eardrums. They could feel me but not touch me. As the rotation continued, I noticed that my coffee was delivered two hours earlier that morning.

Of course, I asked him why he came in so early. Expecting him to give me some crap about having some work to do, I was shocked by his candid response. He told me he wanted to watch me finish my show. After watching his face to see if it was a joke, I reluctantly gave him what he wanted, at least I thought I did. The first song after his arrival did not feel the same but by the second one, I could feel his eyes penetrating me. As his restraint slipped away, he supplanted our mental kiss with a tip-of-the-lust kiss that nearly created a splash within me. As I stood, he moved behind and kissed my neck gently as I teased the listeners. His strong hands gripped my body and found their way to my prominent nipples. He massaged them between his strong fingers as my body language signaled the appropriate amount of pressure. As the song faded, he did not stop as the broadcast became live again. With my gorgeous breasts exposed only to him, my listeners felt what I was feeling. Being careful, I suppressed my sounds of passion to the extent that I could but as the board lit up, I realized that the voyeuristic desires of my audience were trapped inside radio airwaves wishing for sight instead of sound. The slit of my heart-shaped ass was a perfect resting place for his zipped throb. Our bodies played together like smooth jazz as the early stages of his liquid urge manifested in the form of a damp spot on his tailored slacks. Like following the leader, my cradle of life overflowed as subtle sounds of moisture took their place within the storm's music and without missing a beat, sounds of pleasure added moans of passion to the quiet. The inconsistency of my tasty exposure led me to remove my remaining garments. I then removed his shirt while simultaneously sucking on his chest and biting his nipples as he took over my seat. He was in perfect position for me to show him the arch in my back while the tattoo above my ass swayed to the music. I turned and unzipped his raging manhood and with the skill of a streetwalker, I applied a magnum-sized wall of protection with my warm mouth. Even with the barrier, my skills were evident as I tongued his pulsating piece. Just as the song faded, I interrupted his oral paradise to speak some sexy language to my listeners. With every word, I slid further down onto his seemingly neverending manhood. My slow erotic descent felt every powerful vein as my gushing center caused me to utter sounds that would ignite beds all over the city. As my honey-soaked muscles gripped him, the grimace on my face was a testament to strength it took to hold back my feminine release during the show's final hour. With the start of the morning show on the horizon, my quiet storm was anything but quiet as I closed out the show with a body-tingling moan that soaked the airwaves. Right after that, I made one more comment to the listeners my trademark, I moaned, "Thanks for loving me tonight."

As we quickly got dressed, the station manager entered the studio right after the final tuck of clothing. He congratulated me on an outstanding show. As I thanked him and walked away, I wondered two things. Was the station manager among those lusting after me over the airwaves last night and what was the conversation between the two of them after I left?

Over the next year, my show's ratings rocketed to number one. Once again, I owned the market. I noticed that on the weeks when I got my coffee a little earlier, my ratings were higher than normal. I wonder why.

The Entrepreneur

I was on my eighth moneymaking venture in four years. If I thought I could make a legal dollar doing it, I was willing to try it and somehow I always managed to keep a roof over my head and food on my table. Even during lean times when I discovered that the pot of gold promised during the presentations was next to impossible to reach, I pulled the residual together every month like magic and tried to handle my business. I was tired of crossing my fingers hoping that the deposit would outrace the spending. I knew that I needed to change the pattern if I planned to enjoy the rest of my life. Until that change, I continued the pattern because my humble beginning fueled the fire that kept me hustling every day of my life.

Now, I looked just like any other professional woman but I was not your average corporate skirt. Underneath, the fashion plate and the proper grammar was a streetwise hustler with enough education to do the assignment but not the formal document that said I could. The company used that against me like a felony when certain jobs became available. Guess who got to train others to tell me what to do. While the nine to five paid some bills, I used it mainly for benefits.

Actually, I spent some of my time between those hours whispering the benefits of my legitimate hustle to a few of my hungry co-workers. As proud as I am, I never let my work suffer. I worked hard to complete my tasks so I could have more free time to think my way out of their world and create the one I envisioned. My co-workers would always buy something from me just so I could place some type of order for the month. They even started to make jokes about me. My friend once asked me to order her a house, a space ship, and some face cream. After telling her to kiss my butt, we laughed and she placed her usual small order. She knew I was on a mission and she supported me as best she could.

With all that I had done, I still found myself becoming a Jane of all trades and a master of none. The vicious rat race consumed me. All I did was work. I even stopped dating because many of the guys that I would attract found out that by their standards I only looked the part since I did not finish my degree. I let their shallow asses keep stepping and never once thought any less of myself. I guess everyone assumed that I had a strong educational background since I dealt with so many of the company's top executives. Degree or not, I was sure of myself. Another thing I was sure of is that I was starting to get lonely. Now, I didn't want to say that I needed someone to carry some of the mental weight but it sure would have been nice.

One day I went downstairs just to get some fresh air. As I passed the security desk, I stopped to talk to Ray. He was a very nice man and always had a positive word for me. He always jokingly asked me to be his wife. Today was no different. I told him that Ebony White would make me a laughing stock. He laughed as moved towards the elevator to return to work. On my ride up, I thought about him and how he always treated me with kindness and respect. I smiled and thought maybe I should give him a chance. It certainly could not be any worse than what I experienced in the past.

Over the next couple of weeks, my afternoon breaks downstairs became more frequent. I actually started looking forward to them. I think he was too. One day our conversation took a serious turn when he asked if everything was ok. For the first time, I saw a side of him I had not seen. I could see his concern for me in his supportive eyes. He locked out the world and at that moment, I was the only one that mattered. I did everything in my power not to shed a tear but as my eyes filled with wet emotions, a slow race between tears began and my pretty face was the path. Through my blurred vision, I could see the heartbreak in his eyes as his professionalism built a barrier between us. He wanted to make it better but he could not. He was speechless as I once again headed to the elevator.

When I entered the building the next morning, I was embarrassed so I just spoke and kept going. The consistent heartbreak in his eyes made it through the night because his morning look mirrored the last image I saw of him from the previous day. My invisible welcome mat in front of the elevator once again welcomed me to my nine to five. As I walked into the office, I noticed beautiful flowers on the receptionist's desk. She motioned for me to hold on while she finished the call. When she finished, she said, "Ebony, these are for you." I lit up like the morning sun because I really needed to feel something special. I took the flowers and in my mind, I skipped like a little girl to my cubicle. Assuming I knew who sent them, I marched right down to the security desk and said, "Thank you for the flowers." He looked at me with confusion all over his face and replied, "I didn't send you flowers. Why would I do that?" I wanted to leave and never show my face again. Just as I turned to walk away, he called my name with a smile in his voice and I knew then that he was toying with me. I walked back to the desk, thanked him, and gave him a flirtatious punch in the arm for messing with my head. As my guard lowered right before his eyes, he seized the moment, "Let's go out tonight." I replied, "Sure". After agreeing on a time, I walked away wondering where was the man going to take me for dinner.

When I walked into the restaurant, I saw a handsome confident gentleman waiting for me. Thinking he was out of his league, I quickly learned otherwise. My judgmental mindset evaporated as I realized that I was treating him just like those shallow losers use to treat me. As we moved to our corner table in the dimly lit restaurant, the ambiance relaxed me and I felt like a lady with her man. The proximity of our bodies created an image for the onlookers that implied that we were really into each other. My mind beamed as he shared his world and his dreams with me. It was like listening to my own life. The parallels left me shocked and excited about being in the company of my wannabe play- husband.

After finishing our delicious meal, we shared a delectable dessert as our utensils kissed gently in the middle of the sweetness. Underneath the table, the testing brush of my soft foot against his leg without an apology was the catalyst for opening my mind. I removed the shield from my life and gave his attentive ears the eyes to see the real me. He never flinched as my common being found its way to the surface. Over the next few months, our friendship grew as we offered unwavering support to each other. Our pages of life came together like a smooth-flowing book and we were both reading it with the hope that our endings would be the same.

Of all the things that were opened as our handholding journey to each other's deepest emotions continued, my wet love remained closed. Now, do not get me wrong there were many nights when my mental dam used all of its might to hold back the sweet water that rose above my pink banks. I wanted his everything and not just a piece of him. Until things changed, we were both left sizzling for months. He respected all of me.

Love was creeping into our respective actions yet it remained unspoken. Without question, the depths of our emotions cleared a well-lit tunnel of love as the pages of our story lovingly moved towards our next chapter. Between his catering business, my multiple moneymaking ventures, and our respective real jobs, we managed to go back to school. All of his talk about becoming a chef was coming to fruition and my degree completion was on the horizon. Like graduating seniors, we desperately buckled because there was no room for error.

Finally, the moment arrived. We had done it! It was time to celebrate. We decided to return to the restaurant of our initial date. We could hardly enjoy our food because of the overflowing excitement. Our voices moved rapidly as we recounted exciting times during the past year. Our words could not express what we felt. After nibbling our now cold food, we decided to continue the celebration elsewhere.

Before continuing, we had to stop by our office building and pick up something. When we walked into the lobby, he held my hand securely. As he stopped at his workstation, the passion in his eyes hypnotized me as I trembled with anticipation. He lowered himself to one knee presented his platinum dedication to me and said, "Am I worth a laugh?" I replied, with tears in my eyes, "Yes you are Mr. White!" After encircling the correct left one with his first band of love, he stood before me and with gentle kisses wiped away my streaming joy. We were mesmerized as our tongues gently exchanged every ounce of sweetness we felt for each other. At that moment, the heat wave between us torched our lust and left our bodies screaming for relief. I pulled back and gripped his forearms as if to say we have got to stop, but the comforting passionate look in his eyes urged my heart to receive the moment. As I moved to my same daytime spot in front of the elevator, another set of feet shared the space this time. With a ding, the elevator doors opened and with slow sexy steps, I held his hand and for the first time I lead him to me.

When the doors opened to our destination floor, his manly excitement throbbed against my cheeks as his fingers eased into me like a body into a hot bath. With my head turned to the left, I offered him my neck as his soft lips willingly accepted. As we entered the executive conference room, the dimly lit room set the perfect stage for what happened next. I sat him down in a huge leather chair at the end of the lengthy table and took my seat on the opposite end. Feeling powerful, I decided to unlock a deeper side. I asked him to close his eyes until he heard me say, "I love you." Without hesitation, he did so like an obedient sexy servant. With pin-drop silence around us, I said nothing for a couple of minutes. As I shed my skin-thin dress, I slithered onto the long contemporary conference table. My super heroine stance was ready to introduce him to a side of me he had never seen. As the sound of my gorgeous high-heel footsteps on the table approached him, I firmly asked him to take off his shirt. As my approach closed the gap, the power of my position over his reclining body wrapped my mind in leather and placed an imaginary whip in my hand. With a naughty chuckle, I pressed my prickly right heel against the left side of his chest as he released a masculine moan. Sensing his hidden pleasure, I placed my heel directly onto his nipple as our minds simultaneously darkened. His body language said more as his teeth gripped his bottom lip. Being careful not to damage him, I slid my heel to the other side of his chest and followed my mind's footsteps as I repeated the experience. I then removed my shoes and placed my soft feet on his chest and massaged away the remnants of his twisted pleasure with a merciful touch. Quickly reverting to my aggressive mindset, my right foot moved up to his neck and reminded him of the chain of command. As his chest pulsated, his moans filled the room while body honey filled my lady spot. Eyeing the throb in his pants, I released the pressure while his submission remained yet masculine. I could see the desperation on his face as his closed eyes screamed to reopen. Moving to my feet I stood above him and with a firm request, I asked him to remove his pants. As he stood with a soldier's discipline, the fine hair trail from his navel to his waistline wet my mind as my anticipation of seeing and feeling his manhood grew. I moved to the center of the table and extended my body in every direction as my back met the tabletop. I then asked him in a softer voice, "Find me with only your sense of smell." With my eyes now closed, I could hear his bare body slowly moving as his nasal passages crawled over every inch of my body. With patience and skill of surgeon, he mixed his soft tongue and sense of smell to discover every inch of my body. He took me on a journey of ecstasy by not finding me but discovering me. By the time his loving tongue made it to my pink, my body had prepared him an after-work drink because after putting in that kind of work he deserved it. As my body trembled, his tongue met my excited tunnel for the first time. It felt like every nerve in my body gathered at my feminine entrance as each loving tease of tongue pushed my scream closer to his ears. He tongue-loved me unmercifully as a lustful mutiny took place. My mind and body submitted to him. On the heels of my screaming release, my out-of-breath interrupted words made it through to tell him, "I love you." Opening his eyes, he said, "I love you too, every inch of you." I managed to sit up and face him. As we sat face-to-face, I eased onto him and held him tightly with more than my hands as mutual satisfaction exploded within us.

A few months later, he and I walked in on Monday morning and offered our letters of resignation to our respective employers. Stunned by my actions, my employer scrambled to keep me but I declined.

About a month later, the exclusive area near our former employers welcomed its newest restaurant. It was the newest hot spot. One Friday a large boisterous group of professionals was having a great time when one of them asked to give compliments to the chef. The waitress said, "I will get him for you." A few from the group thought it would be great to meet the person who prepared such a fantastic meal. As my husband approached the table to thank them, they were stunned to see the guy they had so often disrespected as a security guard. A familiar but confused voice from the crowd wanted to know who owned the restaurant. Just as my husband answered, "My wife and I own it. As a matter of fact, here she is now." Stepping to his side, I asked the stunned group "Are you enjoying your meal, this evening?"

The Flight Attendant

L ike a crew of secret-wearing models, we divided the awe-struck sea of travelers with each runway-like step. With the fatigue of an early morning pickup weighing us down, the wheels on our bags rotated with an early afternoon pace. Thank goodness those watching could not read our minds, because our minds were screaming get me out of these tight shoes and this damn uniform! The lounge door looked like the entrance to the glory especially after a day of weather delays and re-routes. Quickening our pace, we exploded through the door like excited fans as we finally exhaled. We were now among those like us. After a schedule check, a mailbox check, and a few words in passing to some familiar faces, we were ready to go. Boarding the employee bus, the crew of one married, one single, one who likes her, and even one who likes him headed for our respective land-based lives.

After getting my car from the lot, I called home to let my significant one know I would be there soon. With pillow-longing eyes, I counted the lines on the seemingly endless expressway as my direction moved me further from the airport and closer to my bed. Speaking of bed, that bed has some love waiting for me. Realizing that, the orange hand moved more to the right, as I exceeded law-abiding. Finally, I made it home and my tired sexy body was the only thing that I took out of my vehicle that night. As I opened the door, my barely dressed love greeted me with comfortable arms. As I released a whimpering sigh, my eyes trusted his security as they nearly concluded my night while we were standing in our doorway.

As my bedroom eyes opened slowly to the realization that his loving chest no matter how comfortable could not give me what I needed that night. Exhausted, I used his body as support as we made our way upstairs. As we stepped into the bedroom, his haste to slip into the warm covers was my cue to ready my sweetness for some unpredictable early morning pleasures. His mental erection was visible in his hungering eyes as he watched me slowly peel off my company-issued conservative layer and expose my sweet-scented lace secret. If I would have let him, he would have eaten every skimpy stitch of my matching lace from my tasty body. He extended his hand to me and I reached for his hand but I winked and playfully declined. As his chest pumped with heavy breathing, I showed him no mercy as I flicked my body-scented lace onto the bed and watched him grab it like a next-in-line groom. Instead of reaching for his natural knob, I walked away and reached for the synthetic one so I could feel the touch of hot water loving my body. Never looking back, I imagined his eyes piercing my sexy body as I moved from the darkness of our bedroom and disappeared from his sight. Out of sight but not out of sound, I knew that he could hear my naked footsteps on our bathroom floor. I knew that he could hear the shower door welcome me to a wet caress. I knew that he could hear the cascading water love me from top to bottom and trickle down the drain taking with it the excess heat from my excited skin. As I closed my eyes and accepted the excitement, I could only imagine what my love was doing with the sexy remnants I tossed him a few minutes earlier. What was supposed to be a quick shower double-wet a certain part of me as the blended warm water awakened my pink spot. If I had not opened the shower door when I did, I would have cheated on him with the power of the loving warm water. Knowing that, I rotated the knob to the left as the strength of my water-based lover diminished. Finally, the spaced-out drops of water met the drain as my wet body dripped with anticipation. As the sound of my dainty wet feet met the floor, the naked sound lifted his struggling eyelids long enough for him to see me wrap myself in a towel that probably looked like a mini-dress in his mind. Still wrapped in nothing but a towel, I sat on the bed and began applying my signature scent to my delicious parts. Gripping my toes like lovers holding hands to massaging my shapely legs like a naughty masseuse, I rubbed in my soon-to-be intoxicant as his lusting eyes and diamond-hard piece screamed for mercy. Finally, my natural covering met his underneath the covers. The desperation of his grip said that he missed me. Nearly melting into his body as my face lay on his chest, I was once again reminded that there is no place like home. With our hot skin together after all of the anticipation, my moisture kissed his left thigh as his throb simultaneously brushed against my left thigh. Within minutes of being ready to explode, our bodies lost the battle against the day's numeric illumination and complete exhaustion. I fell asleep on his chest with my left leg overlapping his. Holding each other that night was as sexy as anything we had ever experienced. Well, a couple of months later that all changed.

Given my seniority, I had the privilege having a good schedule every month. I would often take advantage of it by flying to some of my favorite destinations whether working or not. Most of the time, I really enjoyed my career but every now and then on special occasions I would have to miss out on important family events or holidays but I still tried to make the most of it. With summer coming up, I knew it was time to take some time off so he and I could get reacquainted in special way. I picked up some extra hours for a couple of months so I could fund some of my adventurous shopping sprees. Since he had not seen much of me, I was hoping that my new schedule would at least allow me to be off on his birthday. With a silent prayer, I opened the scheduling system and with nervous eyes glanced at the window of time I needed to make his birthday an everlasting memory. Thanks to the scheduling gods, the opportunity was granted.

I immediately checked the seat availability around our special time. It looked excellent for standby travel.

After booking us on the flight and securing a quickie getaway to an all-inclusive resort, the stage was set for what could be the most memorable experience of his life. This time I did not mind sharing my shopping money. When I shared the plan with him, his appreciation was evident as he hugged me tightly and said, "I can't wait." I replied "Neither can I, baby." The mutual excitement struck a chord in us as that caused us to taste a little tongue before he left for work. After our lips said goodbye, I exhaled and curled up in my favorite spot and watched television before calling a few of my fellow crewmembers to check their summer plans. After getting the plans and the carrier's gossip, I had my laughs for the day. Afterwards, I switched gears and took care of some household business since I had a trip coming up the next day. I certainly did not mind the trip because it was just one of my two remaining trips before our quickie getaway. With the house in tip-top shape, I packed my bags and closed my eyes for an early night since I had an early sign-in. Like a machine, I repeated those steps a week later but the work trip was a distant second in my mind. I was focused on the trip after that which had nothing to do with work.

Finally, the day had come. We jumped up like kids on the first day of school because we knew for the next few days all we had to do was think about the ways to enjoy life. As our bodies shared space in the master bathroom, our naked reflections were sexy as hell as they eyed each other in the mirror. Our synchronized brushing put us in rhythm that would not be broken for days. After notifying the neighbors and checking the power switches on appliances, we headed for the airport.

The prelude began on our way to the airport as his curious fingers flipped a wet switch in me thanks to my next-to-nothing skirt. Not to be outdone by his bold display, the windows of the rush hour eighteen-wheelers became the lens to my oral skills as he weaved across the lines like his content was above legal. His moaning nearly drowned out the morning show as I made up for lost time. I worked him to the brink and pulled back with a chuckle as his scowl indicated "What the hell?" I responded, "It's ok, baby. You will need that, later." Desperately trying to regain his composure, he took the airport exit as I tucked away his still-throbbing gift. I was so turned on by now that I did not want to stop teasing him. I spread my legs and gently moved my manicured tips in and out of my tasty pink. With sex burning in my eyes I looked into his starving eyes and wondered if he could think himself back to normal before we made it to baggage check. Impressed by his ability to compose himself, I offered him a sweet fingertip to go with his morning coffee. He savored the flavor.

After checking our bags and making our way to the different-tongued terminal, we took a seat while waiting to board. While sitting there, I watched his excited eyes roam the exterior of several sexy skirts. Knowing him like I do, I was not threatened because he belonged to me. It was actually kind of sexy watching his reaction to others. At one point, I even asked him, much to his surprise, "What do you like about her?" Stunned by my candor, he nervously replied, "She is so sexy!" I replied, "I agree, damn!" Too shocked to say anything with his mouth, his body did the talking as his masculinity once again expanded. I could not help but laugh because I knew he was about to explode. About that time, the screen showed our assigned seats. We were pleased with the seating arrangements.

As we took our first-class seats, a soothing yet different tongue offered us a drink. After we ordered, I said, "There is your girl." Looking like a king on his throne, he sat back and winked at me as if to say watch this. When she returned with the drinks, he said, "We were just talking about how stunning you are." She thanked us and continued working. After we reached cruising altitude, she gave me a note that read, "What did you two really say about me?" Sensing that she knew there was more I nervously wrote back, "We think you are very sexy!" After that, she gave us advice on where we should go when we get to our destination. She also informed us that she lived there and since she did not a have a trip for the next few days she would be more than happy to show us the island. Being cautious, we graciously declined and she understood. The rest of the flight we were treated like royalty thanks to our sexy exotic servant. As we began our initial approach, my mind went back and forth as to whether we should try to reach her while we were there. I finally decided against it. I am sure he would have loved it but he sure as hell wasn't going to tell me that. Honestly, had he told me, I may have said ok. I figured what goes on there stays there. As the landing gear dropped, the desire in her eyes pierced him as if I were not there. Watching the chemistry between the two of them surprised my body with a wet shock. My thin panties could not hold back the joy that eased down the skin of my quivering thighs. The sight of her sexing my man's mind like that drove me wild. I wanted to rip his clothes off right there. Standing on weakened knees to exit the plane, I began a silent countdown because I could not wait to get him to our room and ride his strong hardness until he begged for mercy.

My anticipation grew as the resort elevator reached our floor. After tipping the concierge, he closed our door. As soon as he turned around an affair-like passion overcame me as I pushed him to the bed and devoured him. My crazed heat melted him three times before we left the room.

Several hours later, we showered together and decided to go downstairs to see the resort. We noticed several restaurants, two kinds of beaches, and a massage parlor. We decided to make an appointment for a couples' massage. With additional cost, we could have our massages done on the beach under the stars. I chose the beach massage because I thought it would be romantic. After setting the appointment, we decided to get some rest.

The next day started early for us. After enjoying a native breakfast, we decided to hit the beach for some sun. After walking along the beach, we found a cozy spot and ordered a few cold umbrellas. Ignoring the sun and alcohol rule, we put away enough to release the bees within us. Once again, our room was calling us. On our way back to the room, our slurred language spoke about the anticipation of getting our full-body massage under the Caribbean sky.

After a rejuvenating nap, we cleaned up and headed for the designated area of the beach. We were pleased to find the remote area surrounded by thin partitions on four sides. When we entered the opening, there she was again. Instead, this time she was not wearing her uniform. Her hair flowed as freely as her gorgeous body. Our eyes lusted after her sex appeal as they traveled from her full lips, down to her peeking breasts, and down to her pierced navel. I had to stop looking because I was starting to tingle. About that time, she smiled and said, "This is my second job." Like entranced servants, we took our place on our respective tables as lust blended with the ocean breeze and blew our passion towards the star-filled heavens. Her angelic touch was all that was needed.

When her sweet oiled hands met my skin for the first time, I thought I would explode. Her incredible work became so much more in my mind. As her soft hands caressed the borders of my erogenous zones, she sensed my pleasure and fought to remain professional. As I opened my eyes to see what he was doing while she lovingly massaged me, I found him looking on with intensity that I had never seen. He actually sat up and watched her slither her magic fingers from my head to my toes. By the time she finished, my body's sweet hot tub was overflowing. I wanted to touch myself so badly but somehow I managed to refrain. It was now his turn. Because of his obvious excitement, she had to start him out on his side. Pretending not to be distracted by his massive appreciation for our intimate display, she continued to caress his body with intense skill. Again, my mind did not see it as work. I was even more turned on by her touching him just inches away from sacred places than I was when she wet me. Watching her hands please him with good intentions did mental tricks on me that I did not think were possible. By then, I was so wet that I could not resist the heat of the Caribbean night. I asked her to step outside for a moment. When she left, I joined my husband on his table. After exchanging a passionate tongue with him, I divided my sweetness and eased down onto his throbbing masculinity. My body honey wasted no time blending with his pubic hair because I was so ready for whatever the night would bring. As our rhythmic strokes inched closer to ecstasy, my fingers gripped his chest tightly. In the distance, the faint sounds of reggae could be heard, as our bodies naturally moved to the music. Just as I was about to change my position, I felt soft skin against my back. The next sound I heard was a sweet voice whispering to me saying that she watched our shadows make love while she stood outside. She told me that she had been standing behind me for a few minutes watching me ride him. She moved even closer as her gorgeous breasts melted into my sensitive back. As the patois oozed from her prominent sweet lips, they gently brushed my ear with every sizzling word and my tender spot was on fire. Kneeling behind me and whispering in my ear, she gave me directions on how to make him explode. Between her sexy words and his throb splitting my middle with every stroke, I wanted to scream. As I worked my ass like an exotic dancer, she moved around so I could see her incredible body. When I saw her naked body standing at the end of the table, I thought about how she would ride him if she could. As she showcased her flowing pink divide for me, I could feel my release coming. With the space filled with moans, a chain reaction took place as I exploded with a gushing wetness that weakened me. Before I could fall upon his body, his milk splashed against my heated walls. As for her, she walked over to me and stood face-to-face with her lips nearly touching mine and said, "He will never forget this night." As I stood there with my body on fire, I replied, "I won't either."

The next morning we climbed out of bed and waited for the concierge to take our bags downstairs. We agreed that we had quite a night. As we made it downstairs to the entrance of the resort, a cab was waiting. With the slam of the cab door, our journey home began. On the seat of the cab lay a native newspaper. I thought it would be nice to read it on the way to the airport. As I thumbed through the happenings, I came upon a full-page ad. In the ad was a jaw-dropping beauty. I could not help but laugh. Drawing the attention of my husband and the cab driver our conversation turned to her. According to the driver, Cicely was the most sought after masseuse on the island. He mentioned that he had heard hundreds of breathtaking stories from unsuspecting visitors after their visit with her. Slightly embarrassed, we kept quiet the rest of the ride to the airport. As I peered out the window searching for our special place on the beach, the plane floated into the clouds leaving behind the seductive hands of the flight attendant.

The Gospel Singer

Being blessed with a heavenly voice was not my only asset. My skills extended far beyond the choir stand and there were many around town who knew me only as a secular superstar. On many nights, unnamed faces from the spiritual world would ease into the opposite world and sip on something less than holy water. Obviously embarrassed upon sight, they would tuck their tails and move quickly past those who patted them down earlier. It was funny how those same people who could probably quote the good book verbatim could not just be themselves. I certainly didn't have a problem being myself because there were many mornings when I came straight from the club, grabbed breakfast, and strutted into the sanctuary singing a tune of a different kind.

Going to church on Sunday was nothing new for me since I had been doing it since childhood. In fact, I had deep roots in my place of worship. However, having those roots did not stop the gossip about me from flowing freely through the congregation. After hearing the outrageous rumors for years, I was heart-broken. I could not believe that in a place where love should be overflowing, a hypocritical bulls-eye was placed on my life. Granted, I knew that I was not living their norm, but I had my connection and I just kept living my life. My resilient demeanor finally outlasted the negativity.

One Sunday after being overwhelmed by sweet spiritual sounds, transforming tears eased over the edges of my red eyes and crawled down my face. As talented as I was nothing from my own chords had ever moved me like that day's music. While those standing at their posts moved to assist me, familiar faces looked on with concern. They were concerned about the outcast who so often entertained them in the world. However, only one of those faces moved to assist my emotion-filled body. His take-charge and tender-loving care reversed my emotions. There I was in the middle of service with tears flowing down my face and tears of a different kind flowing from my crying pink. My reaction was indicative of my struggle as I straddled the fence of two kinds of pleasure. Fighting off the sexy urge, I composed myself and enjoyed the rest of the service.

After service, I exchanged greetings with some genuine and not-so-genuine smiles as I made my way to the pastor. As I embraced the pastor, everyone stopped in their tracks just to see what I was going to do. After an appropriate interaction, I headed for the exit. The only thing on my mind at that point was food. With my high heels clicking, I rushed to my car so I could beat the crowd to a popular after-service eatery. Before I could get in my car, I saw the choir director and a few choir members discussing something or someone. I stopped and asked her about joining the choir. She willingly gave me the information as the others looked at me like I had the plague. I thanked her and walked away as the negative rumblings from the others made it to my ears. With every step, I thought about how five years prior, I would have taken my heels off and committed some serious sin but instead I laughed and began singing the day's solo loudly. The looks on their faces were priceless as they listened to my club-trained voice bless the parking lot. As impressed members looked on in amazement, I said to the director, "I will see you on Thursday."

With my stomach now screaming like a shouting member, I sped from the parking lot to add something else to the communion cracker. When I pulled into the restaurant lot, I almost uttered a worldly word when I saw the cars. After creating a space with my small car, I stepped inside the door of the restaurant and stopped in my tracks. The line was nearly out the door. Feeling weak, I leaned against the wall as my eyes traveled from the front of the line to see who was there. In the middle of the line stood the two-faced gentleman whose support in both of my worlds was needed more now than ever. Throwing class out the window, I got his attention with the hope that he would let me break in line. What he did next made me laugh and admire his sense of humor. He motioned for me and said "Honey, what took you so long to get here?" Pretending to be his mate, I replied. "Traffic was terrible." Apparently, he knew that those standing in line behind him would not appreciate my privilege unless I was connected to him.

Given his kindness, I thought the least I could do was buy his dinner. Continuing our role-play and adhering to the sign at the register, I said, "I have cash." After paying, we searched for a table like a real couple.

After finding a seat, we turned back the clock and formally introduced ourselves. Our chat over dinner revealed quite a bit about each other but not everything. Mutually respecting each other, we never mentioned our common world where sex-laden solos took center stage. Before we realized it, we had spent a couple of hours enjoying each other. A mutual need to continue was evident as the words kept flowing from both directions. Finally, standing to leave the restaurant, we made it to the parking lot. Our mutual desire not to appear to be a certain way probably hindered what we really wanted to say as we parted ways. We ended our afternoon with a handshake and the hope to see each other next week.

On my way home, my eyelids did all they could to stay separate. Thank goodness my house was not too far. When I walked in I dropped my purse on the sofa and dropped my body next to it. Like a meaningless ritual, I repeated the routine of turning on the television knowing that within minutes it would be watching me. My sofa embraced my body with a magical touch as it took on the form of my body like a glove. My lipstick was the only thing missing from my church face as my pretty face drifted into slumber. For the next couple of hours my reserved spot had no activity.

Waking from my peaceful sleep, my taste buds longed for something sweet. After enjoying a sweet treat at the kitchen table, I picked my shoes up and headed for my bedroom. Tossing them into my closet with skill of basketball player, I peeled off my borderline Sunday dress. As I walked past the mirror, I glanced at my lace-covered body and found it appealing despite its mild imperfections. Ten pounds since college was not a big deal unless I made it one and I did not. I even went back to the mirror for a second look. This time my roaming hands almost got me into some trouble. Under the guise of a self-exam, I massaged my prominent glands a little longer than necessary. Trying not to make my vow even more difficult, I stopped and shifted my mind to work preparation. Monday was getting closer.

My vow was the most challenging thing I had ever experienced. I needed to hurry and get to the next ministry meeting so I could get some advice on how to deal with my raging womanhood. While I was at work that Monday, things went well. I was filled with goodness and work flowed like a positive river. Not wanting to admit to myself, I thought about my impromptu Sunday dinner date several times throughout the day. I knew that the next time I saw him I was going to ask him the questions that I really wanted answered. One question for sure would be his relationship status. Since I was practically single, I wanted to know. I must have been out of my mind to think about that kind of thing because my vow could be in trouble if he says he is single.

The next evening when I reluctantly took my seat among the large group of single members, my question was answered as he too had his pen ready to take notes on being single on this side of the world. I could not help but wonder as to whether or not he made a vow. My mind almost convinced me to say I hope not. Whew, it was rough on the path at times. After the minister shared some excellent advice, I felt better as my femininity simmered down for the moment. At the end of the session, I patiently waited across the room as eager skirts created reasons to be in his face. When he finished, we moved towards each other like a cheesy commercial in slow motion. At the center of our meeting was common look on our faces that said I am excited to see you here. Not sure what to say to each other, the awkward moment ended with his invitation to a nearby coffee shop. When we got there and sat down with our personal favorites, I sipped one time and asked, "Terry, why are you single?" He looked at me as if to say wow and replied, "That's personal." I responded, "If you didn't want to get personal, you wouldn't be here." After we burst into laughter, he finally told me his full story and I was so glad that it did not involve the same sex. Now, don't get me wrong, I am all for whatever floats your boat as long as that boat doesn't float this way without giving me the privilege of knowing the real deal. After finishing our drinks, we stepped closer to our getting to know each other by exchanging numbers. This time when we walked to our cars our departure ended with a friendly hug. Someone forgot to tell our respective centers that it was a friendly hug because my rising tide seemingly lifted his masculinity beyond my questions about his direction of attraction. His body reinforced his earlier words.

We talked a couple of times over the next couple of days. I even shared that I was going to join the choir. He was excited for me and offered full support. The first time I walked into rehearsal, many from the feminine side looked at me as if I were dirty. Even a few although not nearly as many from the masculine side looked at me the same way. As for those between both sides, they looked at me with warmth as if to say work it, diva! It was easy to where I would get love. After taking my seat, I had to familiarize myself with the words to a few of the songs since I was kind of rusty.

Over the next few months, I learned the words to the choir's trademark songs and blended in much to the chagrin of a shrinking number of empty-life individuals. All the while I was singing myself into good graces, my friend was mentally holding my hand as I transitioned from stages of various smoky environments around town. He and I became very active in the singles' ministry. Through whispers around the church, it was clear that we were becoming quite an item. Within the circle of singles, Jada and Terry became poster children. What the singles did not know was how many times we had fought back the lust on body-gripping nights when the timing was perfect.

In fact, because we nearly burst the seams of lust one night, we tested soon afterwards and shared results. After finding out that our respective pasts had not left an unwanted trace of any kind, we breathed a sigh of relief. We knew that getting tested was the responsible thing to do but I admitted to myself that I may have done it so I could be irresponsible. Based on his actions afterwards, I think he did it for the same reason.

On the Sunday of my solo debut at church, I watched him undress me with his eyes as my borderline dress made the pulpit guests and others sweat. As well as I sang that day, I don't think he heard a word I said, and I don't think he was alone. The contemporary selection allowed me to move parts of me that may not have been visible underneath a robe. As the church leadership stood to praise, I could feel the transformation complete itself. Like club-goers, the entire church stood with an ovation of respect as the regulars became filled with the spirit. What a day, it turned out to be.

Later that evening during a storm, he and I shared a special moment as our relationship took an unexpected turn. As I gave him my undivided attention, he made a move on me. With my dual-purpose dress gripping my body like skin, it proved to be too much because he was one of the few who had seen the dress in my other world. My chameleon-like ability charmed him to the brink of his vow. Knowing both of us had a clean bill, he wanted me more now than ever. The feeling was mutual. He walked behind me and with his hands around my waist, his lips loved the smooth skin of my neck with slow soft kisses. It felt like he was kissing my heart. As I relaxed my body, the warmth from my sweet spot ignited every inch of my body and singed my nerves. I felt like I was melting. The slow but reckless mutual grind caused my short dress to unveil my cheeks as I leaned forward. I could feel his hard lust expand even more as the fabric of his pants held back our naked touch. With my dress raised and my hot pink lace calling his name, I looked back with a wild desire in my eyes. As I turned to him, he lifted me and manhandled me as my back hit the couch and reinvented my reserved spot. This time the couch made room for two as he nearly ripped my dress from my body. Our tongues forcefully wrestled as our lust destroyed our respective vows. His masculine weight on my body reminded me of what I had been missing over the past year. His lips and tongue torched my body with every touch as my sweet honey poured into my skimpy lace. I gripped his body as his silky tongue caused my nipples to mirror his manhood. Sucking me like offspring, he moaned loudly as my body caved in to his sexy ways. As his tongue traveled to my candy-filled region, he absorbed the excess and mopped my walls with his loving tongue. He caused me to sing a tune that not even he had heard. I placed my hand on his head and force-fed him all that he wanted. As my grind intensified, he pulled away and turned me over and firmly placed my head into the corner of the couch. The next feeling caused me to scream as his throbbing desire slid deeply into my snug pink candy. The pain and pleasure of the feeling confused my mind. When I wanted to tell him to stop I couldn't. My mind said no but my body begged for more. After getting used to his strength, I met his grind with an aggressive sway that in a way challenged him to give me more. He stepped up in a big way as our bodies' love zones collided with a splash of hot body water with each stroke. My body trembled as his heat painted my cheeks with wet lust. As he collapsed onto me, our heat blended as our vows ended. For him, his vow of celibacy ended. For me, my vow of not making love to another man ended. You see, what I had not told him was that my choice of music was not my only source of confusion. It was time to move on because waiting twenty years before feeling the touch of another man was more than I could stand. I think Terry finally began to understand why I was often absent from Sunday service during the past year. He continued to support me even though he knew that a couple of times a month, he would have to stare at an empty space in the choir stand, while I peered through the thick glass into the eyes of a numbered jumpsuit. My life of tough decisions continued as my next absence from service signified the eternal absence from my past. With signed papers in hand, I walked away from the thick glass knowing that outside those walls my future was waiting.

The Hairstylist

When I got to work at six o'clock that morning, my clients were already waiting for me. I could not believe I let my girlfriends talk me into doing their hair so early. With my accessories in tow, I dragged my sleepy body over to my soon-to-be filled black chair. With my creative juices flowing, I was ready to create the day's first masterpiece. Instead of staying up late the night before with other juices flowing I should have been resting. I knew that with the holiday weekend coming up a collage of lovely ladies would occupy the seats that day. Eager once-a-month check recipients, polished bi-weekly check recipients and a few feisty every night cash recipients gathered like video girls as they lined the chairs of the shop with heavenly bodies of all flavors. From the bus riders, to co-eds, to corporate skirts, they crossed their legs in the same direction and with dangling shoes added seductive beauty to the shop. With an empty stomach and the taste of toothpaste still fresh in my mouth, I was ready to take on my role of counselor, reporter, confidant, friend and oh yeah, stylist.

As one girlfriend looked on like a star-struck fan, I put the finishing touches on my early morning creation.

That was the one time she finally got quiet. She talked my ear off the entire time while I was working on my other girlfriend's hair. I told her, "You should have been talking to the people at the drive-thru across the street instead of me." After the shop burst into laughter, she offered to grab breakfast for everyone in the shop. I could not have been happier because it gave me a short break before I went into high gear for the day. After we all chatted about the latest news, our final sips of orange juice gave us the collective boost we needed. The assembly line of beauty was in full-effect.

Before our food could digest the shop was filled with an array of beautiful women ready to stretch their beauty to limits. The smell of hot irons and permed hair, blended with a cloud of spray as the busy pace our mouths shouted, whispered, laughed, gossiped, and gave unlicensed advice to anyone who would listen. After vowing several times to not deal with drama, we reneged every time and went right back to it the next day. It was all a part of the mix. The mix of happiness, sadness, anger, rumors, sex, and religion were just a few of the ingredients that went into our tasty dish of life at the salon. Despite the roller coaster of emotions behind those walls we were as tight as glue when it mattered most. We even stuck together on less serious matters such as the poor men who were brave enough to enter our black widow-like world with an inappropriate attitude. Don't get me wrong our regular guys enjoyed a softer side of us because they entered the pink-filled house with respect. Because of that my girls and I would always find a crazy reason to mess with them every time they entered our spot. We talked about our fine delivery guy and how he looked like he could handle a sexy situation. We talked about our sexy product guy and how he could have all of us. We talked about the disappointed box-holding hustlers whose over-priced products could be found for less at the discount store. We even whispered about our own men to the stylist next to us when they would drop by with a personal lunch or a few dollars for the stylist of their choice. A change in facial expressions from all of us when our men would visit signified a watch-yourself kind of attitude. That body language kept us respectful even when we were joking with someone else's guy. Now, when our honored men left, we took a friendly verbal beating from each other. To say we talked noise is an understatement. Even a threat with a hot iron was drowned out by laughter, as the laughing stock could not help but laugh with those laughing at her. It was all in fun because after spending a significant portion of the week with those clowns laughter could not be avoided. Even a few customers had the irons raised from their heads until they composed themselves because no one wanted to be burned while enjoying our unique brand of stand-up comedy.

The long day was finally over and after collapsing into our respective chairs and recapping the day, we slowly collected our personal effects and left the shop together under the protection of love for each other. Under the star-filled sky our tired feet appreciated the comfortable flip-flops as they met the pavement with each step to our vehicles. With mase-laced key chains and a few drive-carefully wishes the interior lights on our cars came to life and welcomed us to our drivers' seats. A couple cars did not allow that luxury but we made sure that all of us were in our cars and moving like a caravan as cell phones alerted our waiting loved-ones. The high-volume sounds of our chosen artists started a front-seat party as we left the dark shop behind for the night.

When I got home, my guy was watching a late game but the game was not nearly as exciting to him as I was. When I sat down, he gave me a sweet kiss and strong hug. His boxers came to hard life as my gentle kiss on his chest made him want to cheer for me instead of his team. I teased him for a couple of minutes before going to take a shower. When I returned wearing some of his boxers I sat down and placed my glass of wine next to his beer. Like a couple of fifty-yard line fans we screamed at the television until the final second disappeared from the scoreboard. We were satisfied with the outcome of the game but we were not yet truly satisfied. There was another game that needed to be played. This game required more involvement from us. As the commentators, put their final touches on the game, we started our touches. Knowing I was tired, he allowed me to relax as he rubbed my face gently. His masculine but gentle hands massaged my neck and shoulders as most of my body relaxed. The one part of me that was not relaxed was my quivering pink heat.

Because that heat would change colors in a few days, I was raging out of control. My relaxed body soon changed its course as his whistle was blown with incredible skill. He twisted like a running back trying to find a hole as my relentless slithering tongue thanked him for the massage. With a pleasing but surprised looked on his face, his eyes shifted to my bouncing breasts as my hot body shielded his line of sight to the television. My naked eclipse outweighed the game's highlights. With my naked ass in full view of the commentators, I wondered what they would have to say if they could see my gaping mounds of flesh moving up and down his sticky manhood. My love water lubricated his vein-filled stiffness as my pink center slid up and down like a long slow kiss. My increasing wet grind sucked the wet lust from his throb as his gentle hands turned rough with a perfectly timed stretch of my cheeks. With his hands occupying my cheeks, my erect breasts met his chest as our kiss topped off our climax. Breathing heavily after the ride, my pleased eyes met his one last time before we finally fell asleep. A couple of hours later, I woke him up as we stumbled from our couch to our bed.

The next morning we got up and shared a nice breakfast before stopping by our place of worship. The traditional members sneaked a peek at us because our sexy tattoos and well-defined bodies disrupted their reason for being there. My strategically placed symbol was the object of desire for many of the suits. I could feel the male heat from the row behind me torch my lower back and reheat the ink in my tattoo every time I stood to praise. As for him, multiple symbols on his defined arms pushed bad-boy fantasies to the surface of many beneath-the-knee skirts. With every request to hug the person next to us, our hugs outnumbered those around us. I even got a few surprising pecks on the cheek from those who knew my face. From hat-wearers to slick young cuties, the feminine members tossed out religion with every chance to hug my handsome man. After getting centered for the week, the rest of our Sunday was filled with good eating and relaxation. Part of that relaxation included live jazz that evening. We stayed out kind of late since the shop was closed on Mondays.

Like most Mondays, I ran errands and cleaned. It was a typical Monday except for my raging inside. The color change was a day closer and I was almost ready to go to his job for lunch. With the exception of a personal touch in the middle of my noon bath, I fought off my begging inside. When he called to tell me that he was going to watch the game at a sports bar after work, I almost cussed him. I wanted to say you need to come and get this now. Understanding that he is a big fan, I said, "Be careful, baby." Hanging up the phone, I popped in a movie, grabbed a bite and turned in early. Waking only to welcome his slight alcohol-scented breath to bed, his boxers snuggled with my sweetness underneath the covers as we secured each other for the night.

Tuesday was the shop's day to catch up on all of the happenings. Because we had fewer clients, we usually had time to relax a little. That Tuesday was different because none of us seemed to be able to relax. Like promiscuous zombies, we were synchronized by nature and all we could talk about that day was how we were going to put it on our men that night. Giving the heat in the shop that day, it was surprising that the delivery guy and the product guy made it out of the shop with their clothes intact. We finally figured out that the monthly calendars were on the same day. I never understood how being in the company of those women could cause such a natural phenomenon. Anyway, I was so ready to take care of my urge. Like kids taking turns, we exchanged graphic details of what we intended to do later that night.

Debra shared how her full lips and silky tongue would make her man beg for mercy. Kim shared how her prominent breasts would sandwich his throbbing heat. Asia told us how she would have her long braids pulled to the limit. Renee shed light on how her thick ass would meet his from-the-back thrust. Mia bragged about how her waxed sweetness would end him early. Before I could share my kinky plan, Patrick walked in and said, "What are you all talking about, today?" Saying nothing, everyone burst into laughter. He looked at me and said jokingly, "Keisha, if you don't tell me, I will cut you off for a month." Fighting to keep a straight face, he laughed along with us. He brought me some fruit so I could have an evening snack while I finished my late evening clients. He told me he would be back in a couple of hours. With a quick kiss he left the heated environment with quickness as his expanding manhood became noticeable. Based on the blushing faces of my girls, they noticed it too. For about five seconds no one said anything until I burst into laughter signaling that it was ok to comment on my man. The others joined me in laughter but limited their comments out of respect for me.

As the others finished and left for the evening, he returned and waited patiently for me to finish my last client. After accepting the cash of my last client, I took a seat in my chair and asked him why he left so fast earlier. Knowing he would not answer me truthfully, I said, "Don't worry about it." After telling him everything that we had talked about that day, I got up and took him by the hand and walked over to Debra's chair. I sat him down and got on my knees and said "Close your eyes and live it, baby." As he closed his eyes, my warm mouth offered his rising piece a sweet resting place as I asked him to say my name. I lathered his piece like an x-rated star. Wondering if he was feeling me, he said, "Suck it, Debra!" Hearing that, I knew he understood. Nearly working him to the limit, I stopped. We moved over to Kim's chair. I sat down and removed my blouse as he placed his throbbing gift between my breasts and worked it with friction. I could hear him say, "Oooh, Kim!" A slight smear of his early satisfaction dotted the space between my breasts. Stopping again, we moved to Asia's chair as I moved into his favorite position and with my hands spreading my cheeks wide, I invited his aggression. His strong manhood started slowly and built a kinky momentum as his hand tested the strength of my honey-blond extensions. Like breaking an out-of- control horse, he controlled me. "Take it, Asia!" He commanded. Feeling his increasing urge, we moved to Renee's chair. Keeping the same position, his thrusts became harder as my cheeks slammed against him with each stroke. My splashing heat soaked every stroke of his ready-to-explode piece. Through a loud moan, he said, "Work that ass, Renee!" Moving to Mia's chair, I spread my glistening pink as my legs dangled over the sides of the chair. Within a minute of entering my available position, he trembled and moaned with the words, "Mia, I wanted you so bad!" By the time the words came out of his mouth, his body spoke to mine in a wet language as we melted together with force. Finally, we made it to my chair and in an almost appropriate position, he knelt before me and kissed my feet as if to say thank you my queen. As I sat back on my symbolic throne, my servant's exhausted body worshipped me because I had given his unspoken fantasy life through me.

The Intern

The face of television's trusted mouths changed significantly as my childhood moved into adulthood. When I was a child, the trusted duo looked more like grandparents. When I became a teenager, the evolution continued as the trusted mouths became distinguished older ones and attractive younger ones. Well, by the time I went from high school to college, the mouths looked more like mine. The evolving mouths of the evening news took on a modern look that reserved the spot that my mind envisioned the day I entered my first speech competition. I knew early in life that behind the dramatic music and the station's signature line my well-articulated words would one day follow with "Welcome to the evening news."

Because of my strong academics and excellent guidance my choices of colleges were many. After weighing all of my options, I decided to attend college in a large city so that I could have more opportunities to sharpen my skills while completing my degree. Granted, there were many potential distractions on the campus but I stayed on track because I knew exactly what I wanted. I realized that I had to complete a few prerequisites before I could get into my major curriculum. The first year and a half was a breeze. I aced the seemingly meaningless courses and continued my academic excellence. As soon as I registered for my fourth semester classes, I headed for the office of my department head. I knew that she had strong ties to the local media since she had taught several of its newscasters. I was so ready to be in the world of the top story. When I walked into her office, I was impressed by this fifty-something statuesque beauty. With an intimidated demeanor, I shook her hand, introduced myself and thanked her for seeing me. Even my confidence took a step back in the presence of Dr. Jocelyn Blake. Sensing my abnormal behavior, she said, "Relax, darling. How can I help you?" Her flamboyant nature was evident in her confusing dialect. I laughed a little because I knew she was from a small town in the south but somehow on her educational path she managed to adopt a dialect that was far from her roots. Anyway, it didn't matter. She was special and I knew she could help me. After sharing my aspirations with her, she told me that I reminded her of herself when she was younger. She even shared a couple of stories about her life experience that made me blush. My level of comfort was high as I laughed and chatted with my new mentor. My comfort level with her was high, but I still did not share any stories about me that might come back to haunt me. Shortly after our instant bonding took place, she gave me the contact information for a local television station anchor. As she shared his information, she lit up like a bubbly schoolgirl and let out a slight moan that made me think she taught him a lesson outside the classroom as well. I could not help but laugh as her wide smile and revealing eyes seemingly confirmed my thoughts. As the well-aged diva stood politely to cue me to leave her, she held both of my hands firmly and said, "Make it happen, Karen." Again, I thanked her and left the office not thinking about my next career move but I left thinking did she really sleep with the city's hottest newscaster. All I knew was that she knew his contact information by heart.

Eager to take advantage of the opportunity, I called him as soon as I got back to the dormitory. My call went to his voicemail. As his recorded sexy voice instructed me, I left a message using my best professional voice and laced it with pillow talk appeal. I knew that when he heard it he would have no problem returning a call to a voice that oozed into the phone lines like sweet warm milk before bedtime. Despite my wishful thinking, I knew that his busy schedule may not have allowed a return call that day no matter how good my recorded appeal sounded. The reality of my typical day once again took center stage as my backpack found its way to my shoulder and led me to the library for a long evening of studying.

The next morning I almost did the unthinkable. I considered missing class just in case he called me. I was so eager to talk with him I called him again between classes. This time I left him my cell phone number. For the sake of not stalking my soon-to-be mentor, I decided to wait for his call. Stretching the truth a little with my professors throughout the day allowed me to keep my phone on while in class as long as it stayed on vibrate. My professors understood. Being a teacher's academic pet probably earned me that privilege. The fact that my mind was not the only beautiful thing about me probably helped as well. In the middle of my two o'clock class my too-expensive-for-a-student handbag vibrated. As I reached into my oversized fashionable bag to check the display screen an unknown number appeared. As I quickly left the classroom and composed myself, I cleared my throat and like a junior version of my adviser, I uttered, "Hello, this is Karen." I had to bite my lip to stop from laughing at myself because I knew I did not normally sound like that. As I listened attentively to his strong voice flowing from his cell phone, I toned down my dramatic speech with one-word responses to let him know that I was following his directions. While putting the final touches on our meeting plans, his voice changed and without letting him know it my listening eased from my eardrums to my panty lines. I figured he was enjoying the conversation for a different reason, but I remained professional. I was so excited the rest of the day I could hardly focus. Obviously, my focus was cloudy because I went to the mall and stretched my plastic even further. I felt like it was worth it because if my meeting with him went well, I would be able to pay for my plastic addiction in a couple of years. Stepping through the mall like I had a job, I picked up the finest professional suit I could find. When I tried it on and looked in the mirror, I looked confident and sexy which is exactly what I wanted. If I looked that delicious to myself I could only imagine how I would look to Mr. Television Man. I figured he would treat me no differently than the trophies I had seen on his arm at professional sporting events and other crowded happenings around the city. Judging by his surface taste in women, his taste buds only appreciated the finest. The anticipation of meeting the object of desire for so many batting lashes left me excited for two reasons. Prioritizing those reasons would be the hard part.

On my way back to campus, I called my advisor to let her know that I had set up a meeting with Rick. Her excitement was evident as she immediately shared unsolicited advice. Respecting her, I kept quiet and listened to the diva. Given her experience, I knew she would not steer me wrong. With one final well wish, my static-filled connection went silent as the call dropped. I rang her back to say a quick thank you. Armed with her sound advice, my intellect and a suit lucky enough to touch my skin, I was ready to make him sweat like it was his first broadcast. After giving myself a dorm room version of a salon treatment, my nails, my feet and my hair beautified me from head to toe. With my suit hanging in a special place above my sexy new shoes, my tired excited eyes lay in bed and watched my attire like security until my watering eyes and lengthy yawn powered me off for the day.

When my alarm went off the next morning, my typical three-snooze rule was broken. My sitting up in bed coincided with his station's early morning newscast. On most mornings, I would miss the top stories because of my three-snooze rule but this morning I wanted to see these hot topics so I could comment on them during my meeting with him. After going to my only morning class, I went back to my room and got dressed for success by adding at least two years to my appearance. Just before I stepped out the door, I applied the sweet scent of my new fragrance that was inspired by my adviser without her knowledge. As I confidently stepped to my vehicle a few of my sorority sisters offered me our signature greeting from across the campus. With a broad smile and a reciprocal greeting, I placed my portfolio in the car and slid in behind it. I was on my way to meet the door to my future.

When I walked into the station lobby and told the receptionist who I was there to see, she looked at me like I was one of his select few. Sensing her obvious envy, I told her that I was a student. I guess that made me safe in her mind so she called him to let him know that I was waiting. As I sat in the lobby looking like a sexy anchorwoman, a few television faces passed through the lobby and offered a cautious smile. I could not believe the odd responses. Just as I was shaking my head and smiling to myself, I opened my eyes and standing in front of me was the man I came to see. I composed myself and stood with a firm handshake. Holding my hand like a grip holding a chord, his hand reluctantly released my soft hand as the remnant of my lotion sweetened his palm. Quickly ushering me to his office, he lost his composure. "You look nice and you smell so good," he said. Pretending to be shocked by his comment, I said, "Thank you, sir. Dr. Blake told me how nice you were." I wanted to remind him of who sent me just to see how he would react. I thought to myself I bet I know why he likes my fragrance. Needless to say, he snapped into professional mode in a hurry. About forty minutes into our meeting, he explained that he would speak with the station manager about me working as his intern. As he closed our meeting with a reluctant release of my soft scented palm, he said, "Expect a call from me by the end of the week." Given his clout, I knew it was a done deal.

After the meeting, he walked me to the reception area and with his consistent confidence he said, "I am looking forward to working you." Ignoring his innuendo, I smiled and corrected his pass at me by saying, "I am looking forward to working with you." I left him wondering if he had a chance as my sweet package strutted through the glass doors on my way to my car. Little did he know I wanted to assault him while we were in his office.

Over the next couple of days, I broke my three-snooze rule, as I made sure I watched the morning show. Finally, the call from him came with the news that I would be starting one week after the semester ended. My mental and physical excitement were at an all time high because soon I would be somewhere near him during the show. With finals on the horizon, I regained my composure and focused on school. After breezing through finals and dancing my way through a few end-of-semester parties, I put on my professional yet inexperienced face and waited for my big day.

When I walked through the door on my first day, the now-comfortable receptionist remembered me and greeted me with a smile. Seemingly seconds after she called his extension, he appeared and again welcomed me with a reluctant release of the corporate grip I offered him. This time even I held on longer to let him know that his body language was being heard loud and clear. As he sauntered past the cubicles of curious eyes, we stopped to greet his co-anchor. Although I had seen her on television, I had never had the pleasure of meeting her. As her in-person beauty battled mine for his lustful attention, I could not help but wonder if he had shared more than a newscast with her. Anyway, she was well put together and definitely fit his taste. After chatting and exchanging materialistic compliments, he quickly brought the dwindling attention back to him and asked me to get him some coffee. Sensing his egotism, I stepped away from the two of them quickly to meet his need but not before offering her a sweet hot beverage. The ambiguous tone of my offer once again temporarily shifted the attention to her. With reciprocal smiles, we locked him out for a moment. When I returned with what happened to be their second cup of the morning, we parted ways as I followed his command around the station for the rest of the day.

Later that week, I decided to take a serious chance with the man who ordered me around the station all week. It was time for me to take control and appeal to another part of his bruised ego that had not drawn me in like he thought it would. I could not let him know he affected me that way until the timing was right. After being asked to come in early on Friday, I figured my responsibilities were about to increase. I was asked to make sure that the notes for the show were in their proper place on the table. While doing so I decided to place a naughty typed note between the pages just before the start of the newscast. I knew that minutes after the countdown to action, he would be shocked and perhaps turned on by my bold request.

After they welcomed the viewers to the morning show and after a weather and traffic report, I knew that my unofficial note that read "I am so attracted to you and I want you to meet me in the office fifteen minutes after the show" would soon surface. Confused by the lack of noticeable response from him, I worked through my disappointment until the show ended. Before I gave up completely, I thought about his lack of response and thought maybe he was just being professional until he got off the set. With that, I continued with my plan.

I went to his office, closed the door, and nervously removed my clothes in anticipation of his arrival. Removing everything from his desk, I replaced his belongings with my tender sexy temple that would belong to him long enough to quell the fire of my anticipation. With my eyes closed and my heart racing, his knob turned as the sound of his opening door made me tremble. I was breathing heavily and trembling when suddenly I felt the kiss of lips softer than mine.

Startled by the soft kiss, I felt it again. My mind urged me to stop but my body would not let me. With my eyes sealed shut for this intimate journey, I allowed the tender moment to evolve. The lipstick barriers did little to stop our eager yet gentle tongues from wrestling passionately. The consistent softness was evident as the gentle hands lovingly massaged my erect nipples. My raunchy mindset eased away as I realized that the touch behind the darkness of my sealed eyes was intent on loving me with a passionate ease. The same warm tongue that slithered its way to my equivalent soul minutes earlier, met my nipples with a body squirming tease that awakened my delicious inside. Coinciding with my opening mind was the opening of my sweet tunnel, as soft fingers multiplied with my body's approval. The slurping sound of creamy fingers joined the slight moans that filled our unfamiliar path. As my wet body language continued, a talented tongue gently painted my inner walls with my own body's cream. As the talented tongue loved me into another position, our connection never ended. The tongue that spoke to the city each morning followed me onto my knees and continued licking me from behind as my gushing grind intensified. A sizzling feeding frenzy was in effect as I spread delicious honey onto the face of the station. Based on the muffled moan my flavor was savored. As I turned around to thank the one who had given me such incredible unexpected pleasure, my nerves were on fire. With my lips just inches away from a new kind of reciprocity, the question came to mind as to how it happened. Suddenly, his office door opened and my question was answered by the stunned look on his face. It looks like we were both expecting him. I just didn't expect my note to end up in the wrong stack!

The Jeweler

Being surrounded by diamonds was no big deal to me. Not only would people come from all over the Big Apple to see my merchandise, they would even leave picture town on the west coast just to get a few pieces for their next red carpet sparkle. While they were in the store many of them admired a smaller yet equally impressive apple when I would step from behind the glass cases. Even with their obvious admiration extending beyond my jewels, my unresponsive body language calmed their over-compensating egos. My clientele was a melting pot of deep-pocket names that were world-renowned. As well versed as I was, my knowledge was limited when it came to certain worlds. My social ignorance was most evident when the oversized clothes entered the shop to add oversized pieces to their image. Since I had grown up in a cookie-cutter neighborhood, anything outside of my sheltered world evoked a handed down response that flowed like a mental chain of misunderstanding from generation to generation. Even my college experience did not remove the barriers from my mind. The fact that I went to a private university that cost more per year than my dad was paying me to run the store probably kept daddy's little gem sheltered too much. There I was an honor graduate with a degree in international business standing behind my father's glass-topped pride and joy helping those with enough money to burn select ridiculously priced ornaments that said I'm so rich!

It was not just my father who placed generational blinders on me. My entire tight-knit community treated all of its young ladies like princesses who would forever be tainted if we made contact with the others. If they had just opened their eyes and minds they would have noticed that within our community even the chosen ones had their share of those with taint potential. Had I told my father that some of his favorites made all kinds of remarks to me before and after I started working at the store, he would have retained my uncle for legal assistance. That legal assistance probably would have been for defense purposes because I am sure he would have hurt one of the surprisingly inappropriate tongues. Anyway, beneath my forced naïve image was an open-minded lady whose wings were pressed against the glass of the rest of the world. I could see the world but I had not spread my wings quite far enough to crack the glass. Shortly after the arrival of the store's most precious piece, the glass case of my world was shattered. The impact left me open in a way I had never been.

I could always tell when some upscale event was about to take place because the calls for the most gaudy pieces doubled. Some of them would ask for the most expensive jewelry in the store just so they could wear it for one night and return it. I guess the wear once and return the next day rule was not exclusive to other communities. The world famous footsteps that entered the store when it was time to impress were often traced by some oversized clothes that in my mind were out of there league. While the rich, recognizable, and famous entered the store with suck-up reception, the baggy clothes were asked "May I help you find something?" until the record broke. After hearing hell no a couple of times, we would step back and observe them like human cameras wearing blue. The fact that a couple of those human cameras in blue found it necessary to linger outside the store whenever they would come around made it ok for me to treat them the same.

One evening while leaning on the counter, the bells on the opening door lifted my attention to a heart-pumping sight. I looked up and three sets of big clothes moved their scowling faces towards mine with a purpose. Shaking like I had been iced, I could not even speak. When the obvious key figure spoke to me in the vernacular of his address, I quickly replied with an outdated response that made them all burst into laughter. After I realized they were shopping for ice and not the princess, I relaxed and reverted to the language that I was accustomed to speaking. The fact that the blue boys were parked in front of the store relaxed me even more.

Over the next few months, a pleasing embrace took place as I began to treat all of my customers with courtesy and respect. In fact, the trio became regular customers as they blended well with the melting pot of cash that rushed into the store get that seemingly priceless piece. Granted, they still stood out but not to me. I even received a platinum chart-topper as a courtesy. Of course, I had no idea what the lyrics meant but the beat was nice. I laughed myself to tears when awe-struck locals would look at me as if to say why is she playing that. One day I pulled up to a light in my two-seater with the top down and increased the volume to bust-an-eardrum level. When I looked over at the car next to me, my stunned mother and father looked as if they had seen a ghost. I sped away as my loud laughter and screeching tires left them in the distance. I could not stop laughing as I ignored the cell phone screen that read "daddy". Knowing he would have something to say about my musical selection, I ignored the calls the rest of the night. I figured he would stop by the store the next day.

Shortly after I opened the store, the bells on the door welcomed my concerned father. Apparently, he forgot that I was an adult. He said he did not want me listening to that kind of music. I looked at him and said, "I am twenty-eight years old, daddy." He quickly got the message and said, "I am just trying to protect you." As we embraced, I felt like his little girl again.

After my father left, Mr. Platinum himself, Y. Nobe, came into the store. This time he was by himself. After exchanging greetings in the vernacular of his zip code, we chatted like old friends. He must have thought I was lost in the conversation because he asked me nearly a dozen times as to whether or not I knew what he was saying. As our conversation shifted to the new pieces that had just arrived, his eyes focused on a piece that excited him like a video girl. It was the most expensive item in our glass. As I watched him mentally become one with the stone, I said nothing. His flawless pronunciation of the rare jewel embarrassed me as I quickly tried to put away the cheat sheet that would have told me everything about the diamond. I could not let him of all people know that I was not as well versed when it came to this spectacular object of his desire. After tucking away my paper knowledge, I thought to myself what happened to his voice. It sure did not sound like the platinum artist I had grown accustomed to seeing in the store. Trying to recover, he quickly snapped back into his hardcore ways and talked about the exclusive piece with tremendous detail. Hearing his rough surface speak about my rare piece of jewelry was the strangest thing I had ever witnessed. What was even stranger was how my sweetness eased down my tunnel while his impressive knowledge controlled the flow with every word. When he finished, he said, "I will own that one day." I wasn't sure if comment was about the rare stone or my sweet inner heaven. The way I felt as he walked away, either way would have been fine with me.

Later that night at my parents, I told my dad that one of our customers knew all about our newest prized possession. Surprised by my revelation my dad said, "I would say fewer than fifty people in the world can speak fluently about that piece. I would love to meet him." "I don't think he is from around here," I cautiously replied. "Did he speak with an accent?" He asked. "Absolutely," I said. Sensing my dad's speculation about my body language, I nearly punctured my lip as my hurried fork made it to my mouth. I wanted that conversation to end immediately.

The next day, the intriguing streetwise know-it-all entered the store just to browse the merchandise. It did not take long for me to figure out that I was the merchandise. As my comfortable body language welcomed his swagger, he said, "Let's go out ma." "Excuse me!" I shouted. Not backing down, he said, "What the deal, ma?" Remembering my changed attitude, I nervously said, "Sure, let's." As his laughter nearly broke the glass, I realized he was laughing at my obvious vocal zip code difference. Blushing, I relaxed with a smile and said, "I would love to go out with you." As his fingers, stroked my numbers into his handheld device, I could not wait for my number to vibrate and solidify our engagement. As his jeans piled at the top of his boots and exited the door, with something between a limp and a swagger, my sweet milk oozed its way down and kissed my lace. My phone stayed in my pocket right next to my tingling yummy the rest of the day.

The vibration came around five o'clock. Still trembling for two reasons, I told him I would be ready in about an hour. Just before six o'clock the bells on the door jingled again as a handsome well-dressed man entered the store. "May I help you, sir?" I asked. "Are you ready?" He replied. After a second look, my gaping mouth was speechless for at least ten seconds. The precious stone standing before me was him. Sporting the area shops' finest on every visible inch, he smiled and opened the door as I slowly walked by him on my way to his car. Like a child staring at a misunderstood object, I slid into his luxury sedan without ever taking my eyes off of him. As I opened his door, I wanted to ask him what happened to his flashy toy with the spinning rims but I had more important questions to ask him. "What in the world happened to you?" I asked. He said with a laugh, "Nothing, I am off work right now." I did not quite understand so he explained it to me. He told me that he was an entertainer and because of the lucrative nature of the business he maximized his earning potential. He compared himself to actors who make the most of their skills by utilizing their talents to make a living. He further explained how he also invested his money wisely to prepare for life beyond the stage. His most stunning revelation came when he told me that he earned a masters degree in business and studied abroad. He also informed me that while studying abroad he developed an interest in diamonds, which explained how he knew so much about the rare rock in our store. As he continued to pull me into his truth with his well-spoken revealing tongue, I wanted to gently suck the tip of cultured tongue and taste all that he had to share. He had my undivided attention as well as my divided attention as my pink trail widened with each revealing step into his world. As his car slowed to a crawl, our conversation shifted to a couple of complaints about traffic and the typical first-date likes and dislikes. That did not last long at all for me because the effect that the jeans turned designer suit had on me was more than I could stand. I asked him to pull over as soon as he could. Thinking that something was wrong, he asked, "Are you ok?" I did not respond so he pulled over with a confused look on his face. He probably thought that I was getting cold feet. He quickly found out that nothing about me was cold.

The look in my eyes said it all as his rising lap understood my actions. As my head disappeared from passers by, my mouth stretched like a boa as my curling tongue discovered his beautiful piece. His diamond-hard acceptance welcomed my out-of-character behavior. As my craving throat expanded to accept every vein, his entertainment image went out the window with every submitting moan. After pulling my hair in an effort to signal surrender, he managed to pry me away from the heartbeat of his lust. Still throbbing, his manhood was controlled by the invisible effects of my silky tongue that was now tucked behind my smeared lipstick. Breathing heavily, I became visible for the passers by just long enough to move to the back seat of his luxurious toy. By the time I got to the back seat, like a high-school jock, he aggressively pulled my designer fabric from my body. There I was in the back seat of his car wearing nothing but my sheltered skin. When his aggressive hands touched my skin, forbidden fantasies filled my mind as his suit disappeared and his roots became my lustful focus. Nothing about that moment needed tenderness. Our avenues of explosive lust intersected as the green light of inhibition allowed us to speed past our minds and crash in the middle of our heated road. As my burning body ignited his skin, the sweaty remnants from each of us kissed with the force of cheaters pressed against time. The back seat of luxury became a sauna of smoking madness as the new car scent blended with the aroma of intoxicating body heat. My body transferred my mind's wildest emotions as his swollen passion entered my zip code's innocence. The street of no-can-do that separated our worlds built a bridge over my sweet gap and drove my wet emotions to an unfamiliar place. The streetlights helped my eyes see his glistening penetration move in and out of my pleasingly aching divide. The sparkle on his impressive jewel was courtesy of my soul's wet gratitude. My nails stamped his back with marks of taboo that would surely remind him of that night during his next shower. Our heavy breathing and steaming bodies blinded the occasional passers by with lust-fogged windows. With the rest of the world shut out, he grinded my pink yummy into submission as my otherwise derogatory language angered his passion for me. He realized that I was playing a role just like he played with his entertainment. In a show of welcomed reciprocity, his otherwise derogatory words, left my inner sweetness pouring out a body language that said take me! He took me on journey that rivaled our ancestral past. The forbidden fruit was willingly devoured. By the time we finished, we had missed our reservation for food. In its place, we had mental nourishment that satisfied our deepest desires.

A couple of months later I told my dad about my relationship with Y. Nobe. Of course, I left out the details of our first date. My dad looked at me with the strangest look and said "Jessica, how would he feel about wearing a yamika instead of a skully in his next video?" With a hearty laugh he hugged me and wished me well. I guess my dad wasn't as out of touch as I thought.

The Kindergarten Teacher

As my body reluctantly rose from the bed, I felt like a student who had broken the school-night ritual and stayed up past bedtime. With the start of the school year upon me, I kissed the summer goodbye. It was time to slip into my morning ritual that would have me at the school and in my classroom awaiting the innocent faces with shirts buttoned all the way to the top. Every year brought a different set of tiny knowledge seekers whose shoes would be scuffed by the end of the day. As my fellow knowledge givers stood outside their respective doors to welcome the backpacks and new clothes, the excitement of day number one had the hallways buzzing. Most of the time I had plenty of energy but for some reason, I felt differently this year. Instead of standing outside exchanging conversation with everyone, I settled into my classroom and forced myself to put on a smiling face as eager parents and children paraded through my melancholy door.

After a couple of years of educating the little ones, my balancing act was a little more difficult since I had little ones of my own. I guess the fact that their handsome seed-giver was often earning frequent-flyer miles to do his part in maintaining our family made my juggling act a little tougher than I would have liked. What was once an effortless ritual placed an unexpected strain on me and left me feeling alone. As my changing body expanded with each flipping month, the fire between my sheets transitioned from a roaring blaze to a flicker. When our family consisted of two, my conjugal passion kissed every room in the house. After doubling the size of the family, my mind magnified his excursions and pushed me deeper into my loneliness. I even allowed speculation of distant lipstick to ease past the gates of my normal thinking. I guess his exhausted behavior fueled the fire of my cloudy thinking. After realizing his pressure-packed priorities, I dismissed my thinking as an exaggerated mental and physical need to feel his love. With the exception of this gap in our desire, we had an outstanding relationship. I did, however, want to express my feelings to him as soon as he could stay in town for more than a day. Since he already appeared to be stressed, I wanted to make sure I brought my feelings to his attention in a calm loving manner.

When he came in from his next trip, I greeted him with a sweet kiss and asked him how long he would be in town. After telling me he would only be home for a couple of days, he moved right upstairs and into his office. Trying to stay calm, I waited a few minutes and let the silence of my mind call him things that involved his mother. There I was standing in the foyer after sweetening his welcome and all he could do was walk past me and go into his office and close the door. Sensing an unpleasant fire starting within me, I did a silent count, collected myself and carefully moved my tired body up the stairs. His behavior although he did not realize it expedited my loving confrontation. As he opened the door after my blunt knock, I forced my happy face to say, "Sweetheart, I need to speak with you as soon as possible." The as-soon-as-possible comment interrupted his corporate demeanor as he quickly transformed into my concerned loving husband.

With his attention focused on my tearing eyes, I told him that I felt so alone. I explained how we used to have so much fun as a couple and as a family. I continued sharing my feelings by telling him that his lack of interest in the woman in me stirred up emotions that I did not want to believe. He said nothing as the heartbreak in his eyes told me that his feelings were embracing mine. When the first tear eased down my cheek, I asked him "Do you still love me?" "Of course, I still love you." He responded. As I continued, I told him that our sexy fire had taken a different course and that our little ones seem to be the focal point. While the fire for our offspring was important, our life before them needed to be rekindled. All the while I was telling him this I could not seem to control my emotions. As my inaudible voice lost the battle to my flooded face of tears, his arms secured me and squeezed me just hard enough not to damage my inside. He pulled back from his embrace and looked beyond his eyes that now mirrored mine and said, "Kerry, you are my wife and my love for you whether seen or unseen will never change." He continued, "I don't ever want you to feel this way again."

Sensing that he was going to correct the disruption to our bliss, my confidence in him dried my tears as my smile replaced them. That night he held me tightly as our normal snuggles were slightly adjusted.

He left for his early morning flight a couple of days later. My eyes barely opened as his mint-laced breath kissed my closed mouth. Thanks to the holiday, I could stay in bed all morning. My increasingly more difficult mornings made that day a special gift from God. As I drifted back into slumber, I took with me the thought that my children would soon be tapping my bedside asking for breakfast. The thought of breakfast made me feel almost as bad as my intention to send them alone to the cabinet for their favorite cereal. When I finally woke up and glanced at the morning numbers, it was after nine o'clock. The fact that I did not hear popular cartoons cracking the windows in my house caused my already emotional mind to panic. Recklessly, jumping out of bed my puffy peds met rose petals that caressed my soles with each step down the path to their ending. At the end of their path was a note that read, "The kids are with the grandparents. Enjoy your day, sweetheart." As if the phone had a hidden camera on me, his perfectly timed call began with "I am not through loving you yet. I will be home tonight."

After reading my precious note again, I decided to go back upstairs and lay out a delicious welcome mat for my guy who had listened so attentively to my heart. For the first time in months, I found the sexy in me. When I tried to find an enticing piece to cover my new found sexy, the fabric stretched to the point of constriction. Finally, I found some incredibly sexy lace to cover my precious extra inches. The last time I wore my choice for that evening, our bed hosted an inferno of miracle creating love. I could not wait for him to get home.

I spent the rest of the day relaxing and trying to ingest some stomach-settling nourishment so our night could be filled with gentle ecstasy. Around six o'clock, our home's security chime pierced my ears as my sweet strength walked through the door. Not quite ready for my night of tender-loving care, my less-than-sexy visual was no problem for him as he embraced me with newlywed intensity. As he kissed me like a forbidden lover, I never felt so much like a woman especially wearing a housecoat. The heat from our wrestling tongues traveled from our lips to our excited centers as his zipped excitement pressed against my joy. As my house slippers stood toe-to-toe with his shiny shoes, I realized that the fire was back and raging out of control. Finally, our kiss came up for air as he took me by the hand and lead me to our bedroom.

When we stepped onto the petals that he left earlier, it reminded me of the sweetness of the entire day. Once again my teary emotions flowed as he laid me next to my expected evening lace that I had planned to slip into later. Based on his actions, I didn't think I would need it. With uncombed new growth, a changing body, and a plain white housecoat, my soul accepted my husband's attraction to my as-is appeal. He placed his hands on my crying face and said, "Today, I took another position with our company." I did not understand so he continued, "I will be working from home and I won't have to travel anymore." Hearing his unselfish news, I replied, "I love you." Before the words could go from his ears to his heart, he kissed me as if I were a virgin. The contrast of his physical action aroused my mental senses and sent a body-shivering message to my already saturated pink candy. He began running his fingers through my new growth. As my body relaxed, he picked up my brush off the nightstand and with an angelic touch, the slow strokes untangled my appearance. I closed my eyes as my face met his lap. For the moment, I lost myself in his quiet loving hands. After he brushed my hair, he lifted it from my neck and massaged my tingling skin. As my body's sexy squirm intensified, his lap hardened and pressed against my face. When I sat up, he removed my housecoat and exposed my changing body and with pride he rubbed my treasure as his obvious happiness sent a tear down his face. As other tears followed, he began to explore every inch of my phenomenal evolution. His hands were followed by soft respectful kisses as kinky took a back seat to this sacred moment. Continuing his pampering ways, he rubbed my feet with spa-like detail. My nerves embraced his gentle advances. The unspoken love in his eyes seemed to say I am sorry for not being here for you. By the time he finished sending his extensions of love throughout my body, I was ready accept his apology in a delicious way. Knowing that I was limited, I positioned myself with my head on my thick soft pillow and invited his stiff desire into my sweet cradle. With the patience of a concerned gynecologist, he probed my special place with extra care. He made sure that nothing would be damaged. With each virgin-appropriate stroke, our careful heat intensified. As our bodies synchronized the rhythm of their considerate actions, our wet emotions united within my sacred tunnel. Making sure that I was ok, he held me tightly as we spooned only this time he had to extend his overlapping arm a little further.

Having my husband home felt incredible but not nearly as incredible as what happened to me next. A couple of months after our passionate night of reassurance, the beauty of a similar night nine months earlier brought Joy to the world. That was my mother's middle name.

The Loan Officer

My reflection of success admired my image as I glanced into the huge glass front of the professional building. As my reflection's eyes surveyed others who had climbed the stairs to the building, it was clear that I was the focal point. My self-admiration was joined by several sets of suited eyes that glared at the hem of my business suit that was just above the backs of my knees. I guess the onlookers forgot I could see them in the glass. Looking like a designers dream, I stepped into the swiveling door and left the haze of my sweet scent behind for the next one lucky enough to occupy the space when it returned for its next passenger. With briefcase in hand, my lipstick branded my cup of hot energy as I nodded a friendly good morning to the radios of protection. "Good morning, Ms. Johnson," said Joe. Moving quickly past their desk, I moved towards the silver doors. The crowded elevator reserved one more space as a nice gentleman held the door and let me squeeze in next to him. His deliberate invasion of my space was not worth the ride. It left me saying, "I should have waited." By the end of that day, I was wishing I had not come at all.

Just like any other morning, things flowed normally. I walked into the office while simultaneously adjusting the setting on my cell phone. It was time to do what I did best, well second best. I sat down in my soothing leather chair as my manicured tip hit the power button on my cyber world. Before going into complete corporate mode, I made a quick call to see what my girls and I were going to do after work. After all, I was single, sexy and financially secure so after work my friends and I just enjoyed the city's hot spots. By the time my screen came up, I abruptly said, "I have to go." With anyone else, my hang up without saying good-bye would have been rude but my friends knew that when duty called I became a financial soldier on a mission to not only get money for others but to get mine as well. After checking e-mail and my tasks for the day, I finished my now warm coffee and waited for the ones in need of my services. When my first call came in, I crossed my legs as one of my physical attributes peeked from underneath my navy skirt. With a whirl of my chair, my professional tone was in full effect as I spoke the language of money. The power of my position boosted my confidence because I was the gateway to the dreams of so many.

Just as my call was ending, I heard commotion outside my door. When I stepped into my doorway, the strength of the hands that grabbed and pushed me against the wall immediately let me know that something was horribly wrong. My potential scream was hushed as my lipstick smeared the inside of his glove. My bulging eyes signified my greatest fear. We were being robbed. As my co-workers and customers lay on the floor, I was forcefully escorted to their side with his hard piece pressed against my body. "If you scream I will hurt you," said the mask. Shaking and crying I adhered to his command. By the time their underhanded act was detected, he and the second mask were long gone. Unable to tell the eager authorities anything, I drove home in a daze after the bank closed for the rest of the day.

The news spread quickly among my loved ones as my cell phone's address book took turns calling me. After a few calls, I stopped taking them and got some much-needed rest so I could clear my mind. As I lay in bed thinking about the unexpected turn of events, my mind revealed a key piece of the puzzle. It occurred to me that the second mask was wearing a fragrance that I recognized. Only people with several zeroes behind their balances could afford that scent. Well, I guess if one held up banks regularly one could afford it. I had only smelled it on two other occasions at high-level industry events. Anyway, I knew that if I smelled it again it would likely stir up some unwanted emotions.

After the investigation turned up nothing, life at the bank returned to normal a few days later. The only difference is that this time extra security was added throughout the building. The rest of my life followed suit as my girls and I soon began painting the town after work. From coffee shops, to martini bars, to fine restaurants, we played hard. Over the next few months, we sweetened the hottest spots with our melting-pot friendship. Maria, Julie, India, and I enjoyed the spotlight of affection everywhere we went as our cash rarely left our purses. The free drinks courtesy of every corner often had us giggling like tipsy teenagers. Rarely did any of the benevolent bartenders, try to break the feminine circle and join our table. Their smiling toast from afar respected us and kept the drink courtesy in perspective. We appreciated that and would usually make those kind gentlemen our dance partners when the music was right.

One night while enjoying the scene, I froze as my concerned friends asked me if everything was ok. "I'm fine," I said. The scent that impacted my money a few months prior was nearby. Not letting them in on my discovery, I slowly looked around and saw the scented sexy specimen dancing right behind me. I quickly turned around and returned to our table. As I sat and watched his body move to the music, his scent was still fresh in my mind. Soon after watching his sexy sway, I envied the position of his dance partner as my mind played a trick on me. I could not believe how my eyes of fear became eyes of lust. I tried to justify my crazy emotions since he was not the one whose hard piece was pressed against my body. As I watched him work the crowd's moist painted lips after his dance, the batting lashes accepted his advances. His mannerisms struck a memory chord as I thought back to the day of my ordeal. His walk was similar to the image on the surveillance tape.

When I got to work the next morning, my flirting earned me the hush-hush privilege to see the surveillance tape again. My analysis of the tape gave me the confidence that he was the second mask. Before, I revealed my thoughts to anyone, I decided to wait awhile and let the investigators continue their efforts. Meanwhile, I had some investigating of my own to do. I continued my routine only this time I added a new piece to the scandalous puzzle. While enjoying our next girls' night out, my first complimentary beverage came from none other than him. His eyes penetrated my eyes' mutual desire from across the room as I savored the flavor of his liquid choice for me. My approving raise of the glass coupled with my coy smile opened the door for his confident approach. When he approached our table and introduced himself, I gave him my middle name "I'm Lynn", I said. He replied, "I'm Jay. Lynn, you look familiar." I responded, "I get that a lot." I wanted to say I bet I do look familiar. Anyway, after dancing the night away we all decided to get a light breakfast and chat. Unless he was an amazing actor, he really did not remember me. Come to think of it, he may not have seen my face that day because he was busy when I was forced to the floor. I guess his possible familiarity with me must have come from the night scene over the past couple of months. As our night ended, we exchanged cell numbers and agreed to talk soon.

A week later, against my better judgment, I decided to go out with him. Surprisingly, I was becoming more comfortable with him despite my initial speculation about him. I kept wondering if and when his dark side would appear. After several more dates over the next couple of months, I allowed him to suck the tip of my tongue a little after each date. The way he did it left my inner woman screaming for more. I was not quite ready to lend myself to his seductive ways. As evidenced by his pressured zipper, I could tell I was not alone in my battle against body-aching lust. This time he was the one with his hard piece pressed against me. On a couple of occasions, after I got home, I opened my naughty little box and caressed my need with my synthetic lover. My controlled ecstasy lasted as long as I could stand it or until the batteries lost power.

Things were going well for us. We were having a good time without any pressure except for the body pressure we felt for each other. Because everything seemed so normal, I relaxed even more. When he picked me up for our date, I got in the car and kissed him with promise. When he put his hand on my leg, I moved it higher so he could discover that I had nothing and I mean nothing to hide. I knew that his mind would be on my candy for the rest of the night. As we pulled into the parking lot of the restaurant, I asked, "Are you hungry?" He looked and said, "The taste I want is not on their menu." Opening the car doors, we made our way to the restaurant. Much to our delight, our reserved table was in a dimly lit corner. While enjoying our meal, we took advantage of every possible way to make food a sensual teasing pleasure. From tying cherry stems with our tongues, to licking excess dessert cream from our lips, we enhanced our anticipation.

When we left the restaurant with our hearts pumping fast, my natural dessert's cream was ready to sweeten his taste even more. Like a getaway driver, he sped away from the lot with his precious cargo. We arrived at his place a few minutes later. As soon as we walked through the door, our tongues met with a tender sweet hunger and wrestled gently as the moans began from both directions. He wasted no time nor did he waste anything else as he knelt before me in his foyer. With my back pressed against his door and my hand placed on the back of his head, I moaned loudly as he licked my candy plate clean. Running like a fountain of liquid gratitude, my body fed his desire until I trembled to the point of submission. He picked me up and carried me over to his king-sized bed. As the weight of his masculinity lay on top of me, I felt his sticky tongue and lips loving my neck as my body squirmed with sizzling pleasure. The direction of his passion made it to my standing nipples as my command guided the appropriate amount of pressure. My body's reaction took over when he found my place. I pushed his head down to my wetness, wrapped my legs around him and locked him into to my world of mouth-watering satisfaction. His talented probing had my pink walls screaming his name. With each swirling lick, my nerves caved in to him. I was so ready to grip his piece. Releasing him from my passionate jail, I pushed him to the bed as he reached for our protective barrier. Once he covered his magnum-sized vein, my moist muscles gripped every inch as I began a slow descent towards his soon-to-be-soaked area. He met my descent with a grind reminiscent of his dance floor moves. As his hands gripped my waist and intensified our body-grinding dance his eyes closed. As he lost himself in the moment, my eyes noticed that his protection drawer was left open. What I saw in the drawer was enough evidence to conclude my personal investigation. As the moaning out-of-control countdown began, the sound of my naked body's skin collapsing upon his chest coincided with our mutually wet release. With our hot bodies pulsating hard and gasping for breath, I whispered in his ear "Would your accomplice really have hurt me that day?" I rose up and waited for his reaction. He was speechless.

Since I only had my skimpy dress to slip over my body, I was dressed in seconds. Apparently, sliding my right foot into my sexy dress sandal while balancing myself did not give him enough time to respond. As I slipped into my other shoe and stood with folded arms his stuttering response did little to convince me that he was not involved. I asked him to take me home. While we were in the car, he explained why he did it. After hearing his story, I ended our relationship but every day I struggle with the thought of changing the status of his loan application that was denied by my predecessor just weeks before our unfortunate day at the bank.

The MD

My encyclopedic knowledge of the human body served my patients well. Because I was one of the best in my area, my patient population increased like Monday morning drug reps in the waiting room. The reason I wanted to become a doctor was so I could help everyone who needed the kind of care people received before the emergence of the insurance wars. While I enjoyed providing the best care, I still needed to survive. In order to live a certain lifestyle and chip away at my mountainous medical school bill, I took on some emergency room assignments a couple of times a month. The emergency room duty injected some excitement into the veins of my routine. One weekend while I was running around the emergency room, I came across a tragic situation that would lead to an injection of a different kind.

When I finished my residency, I worked for a couple of practices in the area. I quickly found out that the inner workings of some of the most well known practices in town had all kinds of problems. I also found out that former business partners turned rivals had a few unpleasant experiences. I didn't know who or what to believe but I knew that I did not want any extra stress. I figured residency provided all the stress and drama I needed so I started my own practice within three years of completing residency. Granted, it was not easy surviving with only a handful of patients. It was even harder to deal with the fact that a hot dog was like a steak in my modest world. I still sometimes wonder how compliant my patients would have been had they known that my diet was worse than their own. Ironically, I educated them on ways to improve their health, while my cost-cutting measures forced me to eat a less than healthy diet. I use to wish I could be in the shoes of some of my medical school classmates who came from wealthy backgrounds but I realized that my promising struggle would make me stronger. My fortitude kept me going until the light at the end of my tunnel was close enough for me to bask in it.

About a year after I started my practice, things were starting to come together. My patient population increased significantly as my waiting room's capacity was tested a couple of times a week. At one point, I thought about hiring a physician's assistant but I opted for a friend of mine who had just completed her nursing degree. She and I had been friends since her days as a medical assistant at one of the practices that I worked for when I finished residency. Her strong work ethic was just what I needed to help my practice run smoothly. Her impact was felt immediately as she took charge of the office. With her there, I could focus on my patients. Since the practice was growing rapidly, I did away with the hot dog menu and enjoyed some fine dining every now and then. Sometimes I would take my nurse to dinner with me after a busy week so we could catch up on each other's personal lives. Because she was married, I didn't take up too much of her personal time. I, on the other hand, had plenty of time to do whatever I wanted. I spent most of my free time sleeping because the most common side effect of emergency room rotations was severe drowsiness. I promised myself I would decrease my hours so I could provide quality care to own patients. Before I could inform the hospital that I was going to decrease my hours, one patient's experience reminded me of why I became a doctor. He needed my care and I gave it to him in many ways.

One Saturday while on the expressway, I was startled by the collective sound of speeding cyclists. Thank goodness, I was alert enough to avoid hitting one of them. As I watched them weave in and out of traffic at incredible speed, I knew that one day I would have the unpleasant task of trying to revive one of those leather-wearing daredevils. Something about speeding down the interstate with nothing but a helmet and leather to protect me wasn't too appealing. However, the courage the riders showed excited me and made me want to ride, just not on the bike. Feeling a rush of my own, I exited the interstate and headed for the hospital parking deck.

When I got to the hospital, I grabbed a cup of coffee so I could make it through my twelve-hour shift. After getting the report, I was ready to take on the busiest trauma center in the city. Like a commander on a battlefield, I led the charge of taking care of the wounded. Although, many of those patients were not my own, they still received the best that I had to offer. Just as I was placing a dressing on a patient's wound, the ramp doors flew open as the gurney sped past me. Just like an hour earlier, the startling speed involved a cyclist. I rushed to assist the paramedics as they updated me on the status of the severely injured patient. It was obvious that he had a leg injury. In an effort to calm his moan, I held his hand tried to get the details of what happened to him. I asked him his name. "I'm Eric," he responded. "Eric, I'm Dr. Mason. What happened?" I asked. After he explained what happened, I decided to look at his leg. Because of his injury, I had to cut his pants to avoid further problems. While cutting his pants from his ankle all the way up to his thigh, I tried to stay focused but his well-defined leg made it next to impossible. I must admit, I purposely angled my cutting towards his groin area so I could get a glimpse of whatever was creating the bulge in his leather. When I discovered that he was not injured as badly as I thought, I created an unnecessary reason to examine the cause of his bulge. I told him that I needed to make sure that he didn't have any nerve damage in the area. "Can you feel that?" I asked as I pressed around his groin area. "Excuse me." I said as my hand brushed against his dormant manhood. After completing my examination, I learned that he had a fractured leg and would need further treatment. He was relieved to find out that his injured leg would at least be fully functional in a few months. After providing him with my special brand of patient care, we chatted for awhile. Apparently, something I said made him think that I would go out with him. I told him that he would be incapacitated for months. He replied "Good, we can just talk and plus I need someone to change my dressing." "What makes you think I would do that for you?" I asked. "Well, if you are the same Dr. Mason, my sister told me about, I expect the best from you." "What is your sister's name?" "Pamela Devine," he answered. I screamed, "Oh my God, she kept saying she was going to introduce us. This is crazy!" Shortly after the revelation, my nurse came rushing into the emergency room to check on her older brother. After she learned that he was ok, she said, "I see you met my brother." All we could do was laugh. Because my sexy new patient was my nurse's brother, I was comfortable adhering to his cocky request.

Soon after we met, he and I began spending time together. It wasn't anything serious but I enjoyed spending time with him. I also enjoyed helping him get back to normal. He acted like such a baby every time I went by to see him. I guess he figured his actions would keep me there longer so he could appreciate my feminine touch. As the weeks passed, he got better and his leg seemed to be healing properly. Every now and then I would test his ability to move the rest of his body by slipping him a little of my sweet medicine. I enjoyed teasing him by dividing my pink lady and easing down onto his pulsating erection. He enjoyed tremendous pleasure by seeing the heartbeat of his lust throb against the entrance of my steamy wetness. As I squatted over my privileged patient, my creamy lust kissed his tip every time I lowered myself onto him. As the veins of his manhood expanded, he was at the mercy of my tease. Because he could not give me the thrust I wanted, I only eased down onto a couple of his strong inches. Whenever I looked back at him, I could tell my sexy repetitions drove him crazy as his aching desire for me reached new heights. I even made him call me doctor a couple times, as I was in total control. Knowing that he was addicted to me, I didn't expose him to my erotic torture on every visit because he had already experienced enough pain.

As he started to move about more, I didn't see as much of him. He was busy with his rehabilitation and I was busy with my practice. I did get a chance to meet him for lunch a couple of times. He looked great and limp was getting better. I figured that within a couple months he would be healthy. The last time I had lunch with him, he told me that he had begun working out again. I told him I would give him a few samples if he needed them for pain after his workout. He agreed to stop by the office the following week to get some samples.

When he came by the office, things didn't go as smoothly as he expected. He saw a side of me that left him confused. I left him standing in his biker suit next to his sister who was just as confused by my cold demeanor as he was. As I knocked on the next patient's door, I told him that I would call him later. I was so pissed I could hardly focus on my patient. The rest of the day, I stayed busy and did not say much to the rest of my staff. My mind was on him and I could not wait until my day ended. When my last patient checked out, I got my keys and left immediately. As soon as I got in my car, I called him to let him know that I was on my way to his place. When I arrived, I walked in, slammed my purse on the couch, and yelled, "I can't believe you got another one of those damn things!" Shocked by my less-than-white-coat behavior, he responded, "Why are you so upset?" I explained to him that people care about him and that they didn't want to lose him. Sensing that I was included in those who did not want to lose him, he tried to calm me with an embrace. It calmed me down enough to listen to him. After understanding his need for speed, I relaxed and urged him to be careful. Intrigued by his adrenaline-laced toy, I walked over to the door that led to his garage. When I opened the door, I saw the most beautiful display of speed and power. As I approached his road-loving chrome-filled rocket, he stood in the doorway and watched me fall in love with it. My hands stroked the metal slowly as I circled the marvelous piece like an exotic dancer preparing to tease. I decided to straddle his crotch rocket. My short skirt rose even higher as I spread my legs to place my sweet center onto the thick leather seat. I could feel the power of the incredible piece of speed as my lady spot came to life. I was so lost in the power of his motorized beast that I nearly forgot he was there. Realizing that his presence was needed to complete my rush, I slowly removed my blouse and turned to him with a wink. With my back arched, I leaned forward to give him a side view of my topless pose. Posing like a naughty cover girl, I eased out of my skirt and removed my shoes. My naked body blended well with the shiny chrome as his approach showed his appreciation for both things of beauty. I could imagine what he felt as his hunger for me intensified. My mind was all over the place as I anticipated a ménage with man and machine. As I gripped the handlebars, my delicious lubricant eased down my pleasure tunnel. When he removed his shirt and joined me on the bike, he enjoyed the rear view that I provided. His voyeuristic moment was interrupted by the sound of his zipper as his jeans unleashed his beautiful piece. I eased back so I could feel the powerful injection of lust make up for the time I teased him. This time I slid all the way down so I could feel every inch of his manly desire. Every time I slid down, I smeared my loving ointment on him and sexually healed him. With his talented tool probing my soaked crevice, my mind weaved in and out of ecstasy. My love-muscle sucked his vein-filled heat until my sweet path ached. As I looked in the rear view mirror, I wiggled my sexy body even more when I saw his grimacing face appreciating the movement of my gaping delight. I knew that he could see our sweet union kissing passionately with every stroke. I was intent on exhausting his hot pipe while we sped down the road of fiery lust. Just as his hands gripped my waist, our wet blend glued us together as our trembling bodies became one. If riding into wind was as exhilarating as the ride we experienced, I could not blame him for wanting to continue. After that night, he and I rode his bike quite a bit, we just never put the key in the ignition.

Acknowledgments

Special thanks to Zahra, Cordelia, Brenda, Bridgette, and Sybrina. You all are the greatest! Also, special thanks to everyone who took the time to read a story or two and give feedback. God bless you! We did it!

Printed in the United States
66449LVS00003B/144